CAUGHT BY SURPRISE

Turning back up the hall, Joaquin saw the first door on the left suddenly open and a naked man step out with a pistol in his hand. He turned and saw Joaquin. The sight of the man in black startled him for a split second. That was all the time Joaquin needed. Swinging the MP-5 up and at the same moment thumbing the selector switch to full automatic, he unleashed the remaining twenty-five rounds of his magazine into the door, the man, and the wall . . .

SPECIAL OPERATIONS COMMAND

JAMES N. PRUITT

BERKLEY BOOKS, NEW YORK

SPECIAL OPERATIONS COMMAND

A Berkley Book / published by arrangement with
the author

PRINTING HISTORY
Berkley edition / June 1990

ISBN: 0-425-12159-3

A BERKLEY BOOK® TM 757,375
Berkley Books are published by The Berkley Publishing Group,
200 Madison Avenue, New York, New York 10016.
The name "BERKLEY" and the "B" logo
are trademarks belonging to Berkley Publishing Corporation.

PRINTED IN THE UNITED STATES OF AMERICA

10   9   8   7   6   5   4   3   2   1

CHAPTER 1

A bolt of lightning shot straight down, as if Thor, the god of thunder and lightning, were target practicing in the open field across the runway. The bright flash was followed by a loud crack and a rumbling echo that made its way across the tarmac with sufficient force to rattle the huge plate glass windows of the airport lounge.

Major B. J. Mattson lifted his drink in a salute to the mythical son of Odin as he watched the rain beat down in a steady rhythm. The thunderstorm had come up quickly, but this was Florida and sudden rainstorms were a common occurrence.

The rain was a fitting end to an already bad day. The morning had started with an argument between him and his wife, Charlotte. This was something that seemed to occur more and more often these days. Sitting at the bar, he tried to remember what they had been fighting about. For once, it hadn't been about his getting out of the service. Maybe that was why he couldn't remember. Charlotte hated military life. The nomad existence, moving from one place to the other, the uncertainty of not knowing when he would be called away at all hours, and most of all, the loneliness that came with B. J. Mattson's chosen profession.

1

He couldn't really blame her. This was far from the life he had promised the good-looking, well-built blonde thirteen years ago. God, had it been that long? It seemed like only yesterday when, at the age of seventeen, he had left home and joined the army, a decision brought on more by the abuse of an alcoholic father than an actual desire to serve his country. His mother had cried and begged him to stay, but he had left from love for her more than anything else. If he had stayed, there would have been trouble between him and his father. He knew he could no longer stand by and watch the man scream and yell at his mother, and even worse would happen if he ever saw his father hit her. That, would have activated the rage that had been building inside him and he would have broken the man in half. That in turn, would have pained his mother to her very soul. So he had left, hoping someday she would understand.

Having been raised in the rugged country of west Texas, B.J. found the rigorous training in the army surprisingly easy and had made that comment to one of his drill instructors. The man had pointed to the cloth jump wings above his left breast pocket and replied, "You think you're such a hard case, Mattson, then get outta this candy-ass leg-army and join some real ass kickers."

B.J. had taken the Sergeant's advice, and after AIT, volunteered for Airborne School at Fort Benning, Georgia. The D.I. hadn't exaggerated. It had been the toughest three weeks of his life. At one point in the second week, he was sure they were out to kill him, but he made it. The day he had his wings pinned on was one of the proudest moments in his life. He was Airborne all the way.

Neither B.J. nor any of his fellow paratroopers of the graduating class of 1968 had any doubt about where they would be assigned. The entire class was bound for The Republic of Vietnam. The Viet Cong had stunned the U.S.

and the world with a surprise attack that spread the entire length of the country within days. American casualties had been high and replacements were needed immediately. It was while awaiting orders that he had his first opportunity to see and meet a real live Green Beret. Barry Sadler, a Green Beret himself, had written and recorded the song about these elite soldiers, and John Wayne had even made a movie about them. Needless to say, when the company commander introduced the six-foot-four, burly sergeant, dressed in tiger-striped fatigues, spit-shined boots, and a perfectly shaped green beret cocked over his left eye, Mattson was impressed.

The Special Forces sergeant had told them they were looking for Green Beret volunteers. He promised nothing but misery and six months of the hardest training in the world. For every fifty men that volunteered for the school, only five would graduate. If any of them felt they had what it took to wear the green beret, they were invited to meet in the cadre classroom that afternoon to take the preselection Special Forces battery test. It was a challenge Mattson couldn't resist.

Over two hundred paratroopers took the test that afternoon. Of that number, only forty had been selected. B. J. Mattson would not be going to Vietnam that year. Instead, he went to Fort Bragg, North Carolina, to the Special Forces School. The first six weeks had been ten times worse than Airborne School. Here he had no doubt they were trying to kill him. Of the original forty men selected, only eighteen remained after those first six weeks.

Next came MOS training. His test scores had shown he had the aptitude to become a Special Forces medic, one of the longest and most demanding of the school's specialties. Mattson met the challenge with the same determination he had demonstrated from his very first week in the army.

After nearly one year of training and schools, he finished in the top two percent of his class. By mid-1970, he found himself in Vietnam as a medic with Special Forces detachment A-102 located at Tien Phuoc in Military Region One. That year the camp had the highest kill ratio of any camp in MR 1, with patrols making contact with the NVA almost every other day. The NVA were suffering an average of fifty to sixty killed per month in engagements with A-102. But those engagements were not all one-sided. Mattson often found himself working on wounded Americans, Vietnamese, and Montagnards around the clock. He saved many in those long hours of work, but many had also been lost. His first tour in Vietnam had been a growing experience for Mattson. He was no longer just a kid from Texas, but a hardened combat soldier: a professional.

When his regular tour was up in 1971, he extended for another six months and took an assignment in Da Nang working with a high-speed Special Forces recon outfit called Command and Control North. Treating the troops in the compound and villagers in the surrounding areas was all well and good, but he longed to go out with the recon teams; that was where the action was. That longing had cost him two bullet holes in one leg and a finger off his left hand. Of the ten-man team that went on that particular mission, six had been killed and four wounded.

B.J. was medevaced back to the States to have a piece of bone grafted in his right leg. By the time he was out of the hospital, the war in Vietnam was winding down and it was time for him to reenlist. He ask for reassignment to Vietnam. The request was denied. The army told him he could reenlist for what they were willing to give him, or he could get out of the army. It was one of the few times he let his temper overrule logic. He told them in no uncertain terms what they could do with their reenlistment and got out.

Within a month after leaving the service, he realized the mistake he'd made. He missed it. Returning home he found little had changed. His dad still drowned himself in a bottle every night and his mother had given up any hope of ever changing the man she had loved for so long. Their life together had deteriorated to nothing more than a marriage of convenience with both parties simply waiting for the end to come. It was more than B.J. could stand. Again he left. This time his mother said nothing, pausing from her knitting only long enough to nod to him as he went out the door. He wished he had taken some time to talk to her that day. Less than one month after he left, both his mother and father were killed when their car ran head-on into a bridge abutment. The highway patrol said his father had enough alcohol in his blood to kill an average man. He buried them both, and sold the house and land. He knew he would never come back to that place.

Taking advantage of the G.I. Bill, he enrolled at Texas A & M in the fall of 1972. His dream of going to medical school and becoming a surgeon had disappeared with the loss of his index finger and permanent bone damage to his hand. He could still use it, but not for the delicate work required of a surgeon. He didn't select a major that first year, opting instead to get the general requirements out of the way. In his second year he became interested in the ROTC program. His time in Special Forces and Vietnam made him a natural leader in the program. His involvement with a part of the army filled him with new life and vigor. He finally had a direction. He would go back into the military, this time as an officer.

B.J. met Charlotte near the end of his second year of school. She was the most beautiful woman he'd ever seen.

Her long, flowing, golden hair; the perfect body that looked as though it had stepped out of a *Playboy* magazine; all combined with a Barbie doll smile that knocked him off his feet. He knew the minute he saw her that she was the woman he wanted to marry and live with forever. He figured getting a date with his dream girl would be easy. After all, he was a good-looking Texas boy with sandy blond hair and a pair of Robert Redford eyes, combined with two hundred pounds of solid muscle packed into a six-foot-four frame. Just like the song said, "He was broad at the shoulders and narrow at the hips." He quickly learned two important things: First, she wasn't as impressed with him as he was with himself; and second, Texas A & M cheerleaders only dated football players.

B. J. Mattson was not a man to admit defeat, no matter what the situation. He was determined to change her mind about him, whatever it took. If she wouldn't date a business major, then how about a football playing business major? After all, he thought, he had been a Green Beret and kept himself in pretty good shape. Even the leg didn't bother him anymore and hell, you didn't need ten fingers to catch a football anyway. He was a walk-in and the coach tried him out. Four long weeks of workouts and three preseason games quickly made him realize he wasn't in as good shape as he thought. The only thing that didn't hurt on his body were his pubic hairs. But B.J. stuck with it and Charlotte even began to smile at him once in a while.

Their first date was to have been after the Texas–Texas A & M game. They spent it at the hospital. B.J. had been a one-man offense against the Longhorns that night. Catching four touchdown passes and totaling three hundred yards receiving. Charlotte had been so thrilled at his performance that she leaped into his arms as he came up the steps of the locker room. He lost his balance and they both tumbled down the stairs. Charlotte wasn't hurt, but B.J. had broken his right leg. At the hospital, Charlotte held his hand and cried. When the doctor came in and told him his football days were over, it was as if a floodgate had opened in her eyes. B.J. held her and told her it was all right. It had been an accident. From that night on, they were inseparable.

They were married in the summer of '75. Charlotte had continued with her classes until their first child was born. It was a boy and they named him Jason. The following year, their daughter Angela was born only two months before B.J. graduated. He not only received his business degree but was also chosen as a Distinguished Military Graduate. With that distinction also came a regular commission to second lieutenant and an assignment back to Special Forces at Fort Bragg.

Charlotte hadn't known much about the military, but B.J. assured her she would love it. There would be a steady paycheck and a chance to travel to different places. At the time, it all sounded so good. The first year at Bragg hadn't been that bad. They had a lot of time together and there had been trips to the ocean which the kids had loved. The trouble really began the third year.

B.J. made first lieutenant and was assigned as the executive officer of a Special Forces A-Team. Charlotte suddenly found herself more and more alone, just her and the kids. B.J. was constantly gone on training missions, some lasting as long as five months. There was travel all right, but B.J. was the only one doing it. By the middle of the fifth year, Charlotte began to talk to him about leaving the service. He could get a better paying job with his business degree and wouldn't have to be gone all the time. By then, B.J. was coming up for promotion to captain. This would give him a chance to have his own A-Team, something he'd always dreamed of. For Charlotte, it only meant he would be working longer hours when he wasn't deployed somewhere around the world. Her patience had just about reached the breaking point. Finally one night she told him either they got out or she was leaving. She'd had all of Fort Bragg she could stand.

Mattson was torn between two loves. He loved Charlotte and couldn't imagine living without her, but he also loved the SF and the job he was doing. There could never be any other job for him. Finally they had compromised. She would stay and he would get them another assignment. Maybe all they needed was a change of scenery. By the summer of '82 they were living in Massachusetts and B.J. was the 10th Special Forces group intelligence officer. The move and the fact that he was home more seemed to calm their troubled marriage. He was still gone occasionally, but never longer than three or four weeks. Charlotte thought they were just more training missions Actually they had been real intelligence-gathering missions into countries such as Liberia, South Yemen, and even a recon mission into North Korea. He felt he hadn't really been deceiving Charlotte; he just didn't want her to worry.

As the formation of the Special Operations Command began to take shape, Mattson's name was mentioned as one of those who could possibly take on the job as assistant SOCOM G-2. His record showed him to be a highly capable and imaginative intelligence officer, which was just what the new organization was going to need.

SOCOM's reassignment orders couldn't have been more timely. Charlotte had once again begun to talk about getting out when the orders for Tampa Bay, Florida, arrived. Along with the orders came a promotion to major. For the first time in their rocky marriage, B.J. heard Charlotte praising the army for something they had done. Florida seemed the perfect solution—for the time being, anyway.

• • •

"Would you care for another drink, sir?"

Mattson was so deep in thought that the voice momentarily startled him. Looking up at the young male bartender dressed in a black vest, white shirt, and a bow tie, he said, "What?"

"Would you care for another Jack Daniel's on the rocks, sir?"

B.J. hadn't realized he had finished the drink. Glancing first at the empty glass, then up at the television monitor that listed the flights, he asked, "Any word on Flight 721 out of Atlanta?"

"No, sir. It's still delayed by the storm front that moved in, but I'm sure they'll be giving its status soon."

Checking the time, he debated whether or not to have another drink. What the hell. It was after 1700 hours and this was Friday. There won't be anyone at the headquarters now anyway. Pushing the glass toward the bartender, he said, "Tell ya what. I've got to make a phone call. Give me another drink, but if you would, take it over to one of those tables in the corner. OK?"

"Yes, sir. No problem. The phones are just to the right as you go out the doors."

"Thank you," said Mattson, as he slid out of his seat and picked up his change from the bar.

Dropping coins in the slot, he punched up the musical tones that connected him with USSOCOM headquarters. The phone was answered on the first ring.

"Headquarters. Special Operations Command. This is not a secure line, Master Sergeant Smith, Staff Duty NCO speaking, sir."

Mattson smiled to himself as he listened to the sergeant's standard telephone procedure. Tommy Smith was the senior crew chief for the aviation wing of SOCOM. Rank didn't mean anything when details such as Staff Duty NCO or Staff Duty Officer came up. Everyone took a turn in the barrel.

Smitty, as he liked to be called by his friends, was a good old boy from Ada, Oklahoma. He had over twenty years in the army and the last five had been with SOCOM. Mattson liked the chief. The man had his shit together.

"Hey there, Smitty. How'd you get stuck with the Friday night desk job?"

Tommy Smith recognized the voice.

"Damned if I know, Major. The sergeant major must've found out it was me who pissed in his coffee last week." Smith could heard a PA system blaring something in the background. "Where you at, Major?"

"Tampa Airport, I'm supposed to pick up some lieutenant commander coming in from Atlanta. Damn storms got everything on delay right now. Thought I'd check in and see if anything was happening."

"Naw. Just the same ol' shit. Everybody started ghostin' out around 1500—Friday, ya know how that goes. Hey, let me ask ya somethin'. Since when'd we start sendin' majors to shuttle people from the airport?"

Mattson laughed.

"Ever since those same majors started showing up at staff meetings without their briefcases and notes." B.J. had been so involved in his argument with Charlotte this morning that he left the case sitting on the dining room table. By the time he realized his mistake, it was too late to go back for it.

"Oh, I get it," snickered Smitty. "Major forgets briefcase, major gets shit detail on Friday afternoon. Right?"

"Something like that, Smitty. The ol' man didn't really have much choice. Our nemesis, General Sweet, hung around after the meeting to see how the ol' man was going to handle my fuck-up. Guess he figured the general sending a major out on a buck sergeant's detail was satisfactory punishment, because the asshole was smiling cheek to cheek when he left the room."

"Was that cheek to cheek smile his ass, or his face? It's hard to tell 'em apart."

Mattson heard a lighter click shut as Smitty continued.

"Listen, Major. When we gonna get rid of that donkey dick? I mean, can't we deep-six his ass somewhere? He sure as hell ain't here to help us. Hell, even you know that, Major."

Mattson wasn't sure how to answer that one. Smitty was right about one thing. Major General Raymond Sweet definitely held no great love for Special Operations, nor for the people involved in it. He had been placed in the command by influential brass in the Pentagon and backed by a select few members of congress who shared Sweet's opinion of Special Operations. The Pentagon boys saw SOCOM as a renegade unit of thrill seekers that threatened to take large chunks out of their appropriations money by requesting expensive high-tech weapons and equipment that would serve only small, combat effective units. The brass preferred million dollar tanks that didn't run and multimillion dollar planes that couldn't get off the ground. They would love nothing better than to see SOCOM fall flat on its face. General Sweet had been placed within the command to watch for any opportunity by which the Special Operations unit could be discredited. The man was a stooge for the mob sitting on their asses in that five-sided building in Arlington, Virginia.

There were even a few politicians who saw the unit as a threat to the United States itself. Some had privately referred to SOCOM as the President's private army. Other more radical officials had appeared on nationally televised talk shows and, walking a fine line between slander and libel, compared the unit to another such special force that had been started in Germany fifty years ago. When pressed by newsmen as to whether or not they were referring to the Nazi SS, these same mallet-heads would either change the subject or refuse to answer. General J. J. Johnson, Commander of SOCOM, knew all about his deputy, General Sweet, but as he had told his staff in Sweet's absence, "Gentlemen, I have no fear of the snake in our house, for I do not intend to give him a reason to bite."

Be it Pentagon brass, politicians, or Sweet, no one but the President controlled SOCOM. If it was destined to die, only he could pull the switch.

"You still there, Major?"

"Yeah, Smitty. I was just considering what you said about Sweet. It's a hell of a tempting thought, but I'm afraid somewhere up the line, somebody would notice they were missing a major general on their game board, even a lowlife like Sweet."

There was a heavy sigh from Smitty's end of the line.

"Yeah. Reckon you're right. It was just a thought for a rainy evening."

"Well, Smitty, I've got to go. Just thought I'd let you know where I am if you need to get in touch. I've got my beeper with me if you need to make contact."

"Yes, sir, I understand. Be sure and bring that new guy by here so we can register and tag him, Major."

"Sure enough, Smitty. See you later."

Mattson went back into the lounge. The boy behind the bar indicated the table where B.J.'s drink was waiting. B.J. nodded his thanks as he sat down. Someone at the bar asked for the television to be turned on. Mattson glanced up from his drink as a familiar voice began the newscast. The face was older, but the voice was just as strong and commanding as the first time B.J. had met the man in Vietnam.

"Good evening. This is Dan Rather reporting." There was the usual three or four second pause that he always used for effect.

"In Afghanistan today, forces of the Mujahideen continued to strengthen their numbers around the beleaguered capital city of Kabul. Afghan government troops have vowed to hold their positions regardless of cost. Ivan Bloskvic, the Soviet delegate to the U.N., has requested an emergency meeting of the security council, claiming that the actions of the Afghan freedom fighters are in direct violation of the agreements of the Russian withdrawal earlier this year."

Mattson slowly shook his head at the statement. When the Russians were slaughtering Afghan men, women, and children they called it "liberation." But when the poor bastards started fighting back and kicking Russian ass, it's called a "violation." Unbelievable.

The next story dealt with another appeal by Oliver North's lawyers. The North case made Mattson sick every time he thought about it. That was one thing about the American public: they sure as hell love their freedom, but brother, how quickly they forget what it costs.

The timing was perfect as Dan continued, "Hope in Central American as the big five meet this week to finalize a permanent declaration of peace. More on this story when we return."

Dan was gone, replaced by some guy talking about his hemorrhoids, when the airport PA system announced, "Ladies and gentlemen, we regret the inconvenience caused by the delays. The weather front is clearing and all flights will begin arriving within the next twenty minutes. Flight 721 from Atlanta will arrive at gate 9. Flights 234 and 831 will be arriving at gates 7 and 8. Thank you for your patience."

B. J. Mattson downed his drink. Placing a ten dollar bill on the table, he stood and waved to the appreciative young man behind the bar.

Lieutenant Commander Jacob Winfield Mortimer IV grinned at the well-built stewardess with the blazing red hair as she made her way up the narrow row of seats. She paused occasionally and, with a pleasing smile enhanced by sparkling white teeth encased in full, tantalizing lips, asked a passenger to place his seat in an upright position. Jake could feel his blood pounding as she neared his section.

He had watched her every move during the flight from Atlanta. He couldn't count the times he had undressed her in his mind. A Harvard graduate mind that, together with his vast knowledge and intimate experiences with women, had quickly calculated her to be a firm 36C in the chest, a trim 25 at the waist, and a solid 35 in the hips. Her back was smooth and curved perfectly down to well-rounded cheeks which strained against her tightly fitting blue skirt. God! She was in perfect condition from stem to stern.

The thought of her lying naked had aroused him to an obvious condition that had not gone unnoticed by the elderly lady in the seat next to him. Trying to appear casual, Jake glanced over at her. She stared blatantly at his crotch, then looked up with a grin and said, "Goodness, sonny. You better ask that young lady out tonight, otherwise I'm afraid you're going to hurt yourself."

The little gray-haired grandmother had managed to accomplish what no other woman had ever been able to do. She had shocked him. He was at a loss for words. Unconsciously, he placed his hands in his lap.

"Is there a problem with your seat belt, sir?"

Jake turned his head back toward the aisle and came face to chest with the 36Cs. The stewardess was bent slightly forward, and he had a perfect view down the front of her white satin blouse. So much for Harvard math. He was staring at a perfectly matched pair of 38s.

She followed his eyes and a small grin appeared at the corner of her mouth. In a sexy, purring voice, she asked, "Do you need some help with your belt, sir?"

Jake detected a slight giggle from grandma, but never took his eyes off the redhead's chest.

"Uh—yes, uh—it seems I may have to let it out a little more. It's kind of tight."

There was the faint scent of spearmint on her breath as she leaned closer and reached for the buckle. As he moved his hands, he noticed a mischievous glint in her eyes as her smile broadened.

"My, my, so I see. That must be awfully uncomfortable."

Her hand brushed against his inner thigh, sending a chill down his back.

"Oh—sorry. These belts can really be difficult sometimes," she said as she kept her hands busy with the buckle and turned her emerald eyes up at him.

She liked what she saw. A ruggedly handsome Navy commander with light blond hair and deep sky blue eyes. The face was golden tan and smooth. The jaw square, but not too much, and there was the cutest little dimple on the left cheek that served to enhance a dazzling smile. She figured him to be maybe thirty or thirty-one. Judging from the broad shoulders and the solid looking muscular arms that strained against the short sleeved shirt of his Navy white uniform, he was anything but a swivel chair officer. They had been exchanging glances ever since he had boarded the plane in Atlanta.

"Are you busy tonight?" he asked.

She finished with the belt, but left her hands in his lap as she answered. "What do you have in mind, sailor?"

"Dinner, dancing, and a few drinks. We'll see where it goes from there. What do you think?"

Her eyes studied him again. She liked him. What was there not to like? she asked herself.

"We'll see," she answered as she straightened up and ran her hands slowly down the front of her skirt to smooth it out, then continued on down the aisle.

The pilot's voice suddenly came over the speaker to announce that they had begun their descent into the Tampa Bay area. Jake leaned out into the aisle and looked to the rear of the plane. "Red" and another stewardess were seated and putting on their seat belts. They both smiled at him. He returned the smile and leaned back in his seat. She hadn't said yes, but then again, she hadn't turned him down, either.

"Don't worry, Commander. She'll go out with you. I saw it in her eyes. Have you been stationed here long?"

Jake turned to the elderly lady and answered, "No. I've been stationed in North Carolina for quite some time. I just received my orders for reassignment to Tampa last week."

"Oh, well, that's nice. You'll just love Florida. It's not as humid and stifling as that North Carolina weather, you know. Oh yes, you're going to like it here, Commander."

Jake simply nodded and laid his head back against the seat.

"Like it, hell!" he thought to himself. If he'd had a choice, he wouldn't be on this airplane. He'd be back at Fort Bragg chugging down a case of beer with the members of his SEAL Team. Why the hell was he in Tampa anyway? And whose bright idea was it to reassign him from the Delta Force to SOCOM? It just didn't make sense. He'd spent the last two years as the Commander of SEAL Team Six for

Christ's sake. SEAL Team Six wasn't just another SEAL Team. It was the Navy component to the U.S. crack anti-terrorist unit The Delta Force. All he could figure was that he had screwed up pretty badly somewhere along the line, but he'd be damned if he could figure out how. The team had been doing one hell of a job for the last eighteen months. There had been two clandestine recons of the Soviet naval facilities off the coast of Kaliningrad and two other operations around the harbors of Puerto Somoza and Corinto in Nicaragua. Add those together with a six month training mission in El Salvador teaching underwater demolitions and tactics and you had a pretty good idea of how well the team had been working. USSOCOM had to know that. They were the ones who had ordered the Russian and Nicaraguan operations.

No, sir. No matter how many ways he tried to look at the situation, it still didn't make sense. Why take an experienced commander out of a line unit and assign him to a headquarters? If he wanted a desk job he would have stayed in Philadelphia and worked in his father's law firm. Not only was it one of the most prestigious law offices in the country, but also one of the oldest. Founded by his great-great grandfather before the start of the Revolutionary War. The Mortimer name was Philadelphia Main Line. The family had accumulated a fortune so vast that it could easily provide a life of luxury for the next three generations of Mortimer bluebloods. The idea that one of their sons would actually turn his back on that fortune had stunned the entire family.

His grandmother insisted that four years of playing football when he was at Harvard had caused brain damage. When he had joined the Navy the rest of the family began to think grandmama was right.

Jacob Winfield Mortimer IV was anything but brain

damaged. When most kids were graduating from high school, Jake Mortimer had been completing his sophomore year at Harvard. By the age of twenty he had graduated from one of the most prestigious colleges in America. That was when he dropped the bombshell on the family and applied for and was accepted to the U.S. Naval Academy at Annapolis. Jake had loved the Academy and had never once regretted his career decision. As he had done at Harvard, Jacob Mortimer graduated in the top five percent of his class, a feat which did not go unrewarded by the Navy Department. Jake's academic achievements were of such high standards that upon the recommendation of both the Academy and the Navy Department, he had been commissioned a lieutenant junior grade rather than an ensign.

That had been eight years ago. Since then, there had been Airborne School, SEAL School, advanced weapons and demolitions courses, as well as Intelligence School; Missions in Nicaragua, El Salvador, the Russian coast, and the Middle East. It was a rough and rugged road, but Jake loved every minute of it. When his fellow officers asked him why he kept knocking himself out by taking on the toughest combat schools, Jake had allowed a well-hidden side of his character to emerge in his answer. In his opinion, the Vietnam War had been lost by incompetent officers who had demanded more of their men than they themselves were capable of giving. They were "losers"—and that was something no one would ever be able to say about Jake Mortimer.

A state of depression began to edge its way into his thoughts. In his twelve-year involvement with the military this was the first time he had ever considered resigning. Of course, that would be a decision which was sure to please the family. His father had placed Jake's name on an office door of the firm twelve years ago. It was still there. He tried to shake the mood as he felt the aircraft begin its descent, but it wouldn't go away. If they tried to stick him with a desk job, he would file the necessary papers and resign. If nothing else, the long plane ride wouldn't be a total loss. There was still the lovely stewardess.

Jake Mortimer stood patiently waiting for his luggage to come down the chute. Outside, the rain had stopped and the sky was clearing as twilight approached. Unfolding the small piece of paper that "Red" had passed to him as he left the plane, he smiled to himself as he read the flawless handwriting.

Karen Davis
Residence Inn Tampa Airport, Suite 202
3075 North Rocky Point Drive East
887–5576
I should be home by eight. Give me a call.

The note had already put him in a better mood. Maybe this Florida business wouldn't be such a bad deal after all. Spotting his two large, gray suitcases coming around on the carousel, he reached down and grabbed one and was reaching for the other, when a voice behind him asked, "That other one yours, too?"

Mortimer turned and stared up at the tall major in Class A dress uniform. On the right were an impressive number of combat ribbons, topped off by a combat infantryman's badge, and above that, a highly shined pair of U.S. jump wings. On the left side were unit citations and a black plastic name tag that read, "Mattson."

Without waiting for Mortimer's reply, Mattson snatched up the other gray bag.

"Figure they're a matched set," said Mattson as he glanced at Jake's name tag on the Navy dress whites. "Jacob Mortimer, I presume."

Mortimer was still studying the rows of combat ribbons, noting that the first two at the top were the Distinguished Service Cross and the Silver Star. The only award higher than those two was the Medal of Honor. "Yes, I'm Lieutenant Commander Mortimer."

Mattson switched the suitcase to his left and reached out with his right. "Major B. J. Mattson, USSOCOM Assistant G-2. I'm here to pick you up and help you get squared away."

"Thank you, Major. The two bags are all I brought with me. The rest of my things should arrive at the transportation office in a few days."

"Fine, Commander. If you'll come with me, my car's out front. We'll get you over to HQ and get you signed in."

"Of course," said Jake. He fell in alongside Mattson as they left the airport and walked across the parking lot.

Placing the bags in the trunk of the staff car, they both slid into the front seat. As Mortimer buckled his seat belt, he asked, "How long have you been with USSOCOM, Major Mattson?"

"Since early '86," said B.J. as he started up the car and headed out of the terminal.

Mortimer thought for a moment, then said, "I didn't think they activated USSOCOM until April of '87."

"You're right. That was the official date. But we'd been planning it a lot longer than that. By the time the man in the White House got approval from congress we were ready. We took over the former U.S. Readiness Command facilities and utilized some of their people. I guess you'd say I got in on the ground floor."

Jake noted the Special Forces Combat patch on the right shoulder of B.J.'s uniform. "You have much time in SF?"

"Four years as an NCO. Did some time in Nam. Got out and went to Texas A & M, got my degree, then back to SF.

Been with 'em almost thirteen years this trip. Wouldn't want to be anywhere else."

"Well, let me ask you something then, Major."

"Call me B.J., Commander. 'Major' sounds so damn formal."

"OK, B.J. You're the G-2. Can you tell me why in hell I'm here?"

Mattson grinned as he said, "Wondering what a SEAL Team line commander is doing in paper shuffle land are we?"

"You got it."

"Well that makes two of us then. All I know is ol' Q-Tip wanted you here and here you are. Told us to pull the records on all SEAL Team leaders and bring them to his office. That was last week sometime. Guess you were the lucky winner. Whatever the ol' man's got in mind, he's keeping to himself. But whatever it is, you can bet your PT boat it won't have anything to do with shuffling papers."

Mortimer sighed in relief at the last part of Mattson's statement. Thank God it wasn't going to be a staff job.

"Major—or—I mean, B.J. You said, 'Q-Tip.' Are we talking about General Johnson?"

Mattson laughed. "Yeah. That's what the boys down here call him. Surprised you've never met him."

"No. As a matter of fact, I've been working for him for over two years now and never laid eyes on him. Every time he was at Fort Bragg, or out at the Navy Special Ops Command in Coronado, my team and I were deployed. They say he's a real hell-raiser and a firm believer in Specials Operations."

"You better believe it. You know the President personally picked him to run USSOCOM. Didn't even consider anyone else for the job. The ol' man's hair is whiter than new Alaskan snow. Some of the boys say it got that way from flying a record number of combat missions in Vietnam. The general can fly just about anything with wings or a rotor blade on it. Others say his hair bleached out the day the President told him to report to the White House. And brother, they're right about one thing: He's as hard as a dinosaur's toenails, but he's a fair man, too."

Jake laughed as he leaned back in the seat. "Now I'd say that's some kind of hard."

Mortimer relaxed as they drove along West Shore Boulevard. Flickering neon lights were coming to life all over the city, as twilight began to close in on Tampa. A billboard along the side of the highway caught Jake's attention: "Tampa Bay, Home of the Tampa Bay Buccaneers." Maybe, just maybe this wasn't going to be such a bad assignment after all.

As they approached the main gate of MacDill Air Force Base, B.J. pulled out his ID card and told Mortimer to do the same. The guard checked them out, then waved them through the gate. Two F-16s lifted off in tandem, the roar of their mighty engines disappearing into the night sky.

Driving down Tampa Boulevard, B.J. swung the car in front of the USSOCOM headquarters building and parked. It wasn't at all what Mortimer had expected. It was a long, two-story, white structure. The sign in front was a simple white slab affair with the words, "United States Special Operations Command." Two flowing palm trees stood at each end of the sign.

"Not quite what you counted on, is it?"

"No. Guess after seeing that eight-story puzzle palace at Fort Bragg, I was expecting a skyscraper."

"Well, she isn't the tallest building in Tampa, but ol' Q-Tip has control of over thirty-five thousand men from here. Like the commercial says, he just picks up the phone to reach out and touch someone."

Both men stepped from the car and went inside. Master Sergeant Tommy Smith sat at the staff duty desk. Jake figured the sergeant to be about five-foot-ten, but he was built like a brick wall.

"Hi, ya, Major. See you found our new arrival," said Smith as he stuck his big hand out to Mortimer. Jake shook hands and was surprised at the amount of strength in the man's grip.

"Well, Commander, if you'll just sign the incoming personnel book and give me three copies of your orders, I'll be done with ya and you and the major can head to the club for a drink."

"Best offer I've had since I left Fort Bragg," said Mortimer.

While Jake signed in, Smith pulled B.J. to one side and in a low voice said, "Sir, Charlotte called 'bout half an hour ago. I told her what was goin' on, about you pickin' up the commander and all. She wanted me to tell ya that she was goin' out to dinner tonight with Captain Anderson's wife. Nancy's got the kids over at our house. They done had supper and they're watchin' some movies she got from the video store. Your kids wanted to know if they could stay overnight and play. I told Nancy I'd ask you when you brought the commander in. It really ain't no problem, B.J."

"Goddamnit," whispered Mattson under his breath. Charlotte was doing this to get back at him for their argument this morning. She knew how he felt about Sue Anderson. The woman was on the verge of becoming a full-fledged alcoholic and her reputation around the base had quickly become the topic of whispered conversations. Charlotte refused to believe the rumors. Besides they had something in common; they shared a dislike for the military. What bothered him even more was the fact that Flight

Officer Larry Anderson was attending Language School in California and wouldn't be home for three more months.

"Will that be all right, B.J.?" asked Smith.

"Sure, Smitty. As long as you and Nancy don't mind."

Smith nodded and returned to the desk. He and Nancy had known Charlotte and B.J. for over three years. They were all close friends and he could tell that B.J. was worried about Charlotte being out with Sue Anderson.

"That should do it, Sergeant Smith," said Jake as he closed the book.

Reaching into the desk drawer, Smith brought out a key and gave it to Mortimer.

"Here's your room key, sir, number 15 at the visitor's officers' quarters. That should do ya over the weekend, until we can get somethin' more permanent on Monday. Well, reckon y'all are free to head to the ol' waterin' hole, Major."

"Thanks, Smitty. For everything. Commander, you feel up to lifting a few before I drop you off at the Q?"

"Sounds good to me. Point the way. Thanks, Sergeant Smith," said Jake as the two officers left. Tommy nodded and waved as he picked up the phone to call his wife.

The main ballroom bar was already crowded. B.J. led Jake through the mob to a smaller stag bar that sat off the main floor. Country music played on the jukebox. They found two seats at the far end of the bar. As they waited for their drinks, Jake looked at the medals on Mattson's uniform again. "You say you were an enlisted man before you became an officer, B.J."

"Yeah. SF medic. Made staff sergeant in four years."

"How long did you have to stay in Vietnam to get all that fruit salad?"

"Almost got two years of it. Got hit running recon. They

wouldn't let me go back, so I got out. Ruined a hell of a promising career as a surgeon too," said B.J. as he held up a hand with a missing finger and badly scarred palm. Jake had been with Mattson two hours and hadn't even noticed the hand.

The waiter brought their drinks. B.J. lifted his glass in a toast.

"Well, Commander, as the only official welcoming party for this fine organization, I welcome you to the United States Special Operations Command."

Jake tapped his glass with Mattson's and took a hearty drink of scotch and water. Jake found himself a little confused about his opinion of the Vietnam "losers," as he called them. Judging from the awards on B.J.'s chest the major was anything but a loser. As a matter of fact, he seemed like a damn likable guy. He wanted to ask about the DSC award but not right now, maybe later, after they had worked together for a while.

Mattson spent the next hour giving Jake a rundown on the missions and operations they were expected to handle at USSOCOM. Basically what it meant was that whenever a problem or situation developed anywhere in the world involving American personnel or American interests, the President or the Secretary of Defense would alert General Johnson to the potential situation and request that USSO-COM correct the problem before it got out of hand. Johnson had at his command the Green Berets from 1st Special Operations Command at Fort Bragg, North Carolina, Navy SEALs from the Naval Special Operations Command, in Coronado, California, as well as the 23rd Air Force, Air Special Operations Command out of Hurlburt Field in Florida. The general could pick any one of these units or a mix-match of all three, depending on what the mission requirement might be.

Jake had started to ask a question when B.J.'s beeper sounded.

"Looks like I have a call. Order us another round and I'll be right back." Mattson slid out of his chair and headed for the lobby.

Jake caught the bartender's attention and signaled for two more drinks. As he waited, he happened to glance up at the clock behind the bar. Damn! He had forgotten to call Karen at eight. It was already past ten o'clock. Rushing out to the lobby, he pulled the paper from his shirt pocket and dialed the number. How could he have forgotten a body like that? The phone rang twice before the answering machine clicked on.

"Hi, this is Karen. I'm not in right now, but if you will leave your name and number at the tone, I'll return your call as soon as possible. Thank you. Bye-bye."

There was a five-second pause, then a beep.

"Karen. This is Jake Mortimer. Sorry about tonight, but I got tied up with business. I'll call again tomorrow. Again, I'm sorry. Bye."

Hanging up the phone, Jake considered his chances for another shot. If that redhead had a temper to match her hair he was shit out of luck. Turning the paper over, he made a note. "Send two dozen roses to Karen first thing A.M." Replacing the paper in his pocket, he went back to the bar. B.J. was already back.

"Was the call important?" asked Jake.

"Yeah. That was Sergeant Smith. Hope you didn't have any plans for early in the morning."

Jake took a sip of his drink and said, "Well, nothing real early. What's up?"

"I'm not sure. Like I said, the ol' man plays his cards close to the vest. But I have a feeling we might just find out what you're doing here. We're supposed to meet him at the Rocky Point Country Club at 0700 in the morning."

"Anything strange about that?"

"Hard to say. But whatever he wants to talk about, he doesn't want anybody around here seeing the three of us together. Rocky Point Golf Course is a civilian outfit near the airport where I picked you up. What's that tell you?"

Jake peered over the top of his glass at Mattson. The cute little dimple that Karen admired so much suddenly appeared as he grinned and whispered, "Sweet."

B.J. tipped his glass to Jake as he replied, "By George! I think you've got it." They both broke out with a laugh at the same time. Jake waved for another round. Tomorrow was tomorrow. For now it was party time. As the drinks arrived, other members of the SOCOM staff gathered around to meet the newest member of their elite group. B.J. made the introductions, then stepped to the side of the bar and looked up at the clock. He wondered if Charlotte was home yet.

CHAPTER 2

The sun had set beyond the Andean Mountains as the merchants of the oil rich boom town of Lago Agrio, Ecuador, began closing their shops. In the market square and along side streets, the Indians and the farmers of the mountain villages loaded their unsold vegetables and fruit into woven straw baskets and hoisted them on their backs. Slipping tired arms through improvised shoulder straps made of tree bark, they began their long trek back up the hillsides to home.

With the rapidly fading sunlight came a sudden drop in temperature. A fine ground mist, much like a London fog, began to creep and spread its way up the Santa Cecilla Valley and along the streets of Lago Agrio.

The eerie fog was a routine summer visitor to many of the towns and villages that lay along the equator. During the day the temperatures were warm to hot, but with the disappearing sun came cold westerly breezes from the snowcapped mountains of the Andes. The combination of cool air and still warm earth gave birth to the knee-high fog that now snaked its way through the streets and alleyways. The common occurrence went unnoticed by the residents of the town. Little did they know that, on this night, the fog had not come alone. With it had come death; death in the form of men dressed in black and carrying with them weapons of destruction.

The five men moved along the narrow streets as if they were themselves the shadows of each building. Slowly, with disciplined precision, they made their way beyond the marketplace and across the main thoroughfare of Lavdio Avenue. They were now in the residential area of the more affluent members of Lago Agrio's ruling class. Moving along the edges of neatly landscaped lawns, the group suddenly stopped as the headlights of an approaching car rounded the corner at the end of the street. There was no panic or sudden scramble for cover, but rather, a slow, precise movement by all five men at the same moment. They melted into the shadows of the trees and hedges. As the car passed, they reemerged and continued their silent advance.

They crossed another street, then down another block, and into a heavily wooded area. The tallest of the five men was in the lead. Reaching the edge of the woods, he slowly raised his hand and halted the team. Listening intently for a few seconds, he slowly lowered himself down on one knee. The others quietly did the same. Signaling for the others to stay, the tall one moved forward and parted the low hanging branches of a kapok tree. Through the small opening he could see the large double wrought iron gates that blocked the entrance to the villa across the street. Three Ecuadorian soldiers armed with M-16 automatic rifles, guarded the entrance.

The gates were connected to a ten foot brick wall that surrounded the elegant colonial mansion. Spotlights were positioned to the left and right of the gates, with other lights located every twenty yards along the top of the entire wall. The silent observer let his eyes roam along the top until they found what he was searching for. Just beyond the faint edges of the gate lights were two remote cameras that continuously scanned the area from the gate entrance to each end of the street and back again. If their intelligence was correct, and so far it had been flawless, there would be two more soldiers in each of the guard positions at the four corners of the outside wall. Inside there should be a private security force of ten men that lived on the estate. They worked the night duty in two shifts of five men each, three hours on, three hours off. It was this security force that presented the real threat to the mission. The interior guards had no set pattern of movement around the grounds. An accidental encounter could mean compromise and mission failure. They would have to patiently search out and neutralize the five security people before making their move on the house.

Slowly, and with painstaking care, Joaquin Ochoa, the Cuban leader of the five-man group of night raiders, released the branches and inched himself back to where the others waited. Lifting the back of his black glove, he checked the time on his illuminated watch. It was only nine-thirty. Their progress up the valley and through the town had gone more easily than expected. They were ahead of schedule. Looking up at his four comrades, Ochoa held up two fingers and whispered, "Dos horas—descanso."

The men nodded in the darkness and with cat-like movements, eased themselves into comfortable positions against the trees, grateful for the opportunity of two hours' rest.

Ochoa returned to his vantage point at the edge of the trees. The three guards were now sitting on the sidewalk with their backs against the wall. Joaquin smiled to himself. Even this behavior had been noted in the detailed intelligence briefing he had received less than twenty-four hours ago from Colonel Suplao, his commander. It had been a very detailed briefing indeed.

"Security for the governor's estate is provided by a company of the Ecuadorian Armies, 3rd Brigade. Their primary mission is the security of the oil pumping stations and pipelines leading out of Lago Agrio. One platoon is detailed on a weekly rotating basis to provide security at the estate. The 3rd has been stationed in the town for over three months and the unit has become complacent due to boredom and inactivity. Attention to detail and alertness are next to nonexistent. Not only among the enlisted personnel, but the officers as well. The guards at the main gate have a tendency to take sitting positions against the wall, after being checked by the officer of the guard at ten o'clock. By eleven or eleven-thirty, nearly all the guards are asleep."

Ochoa would see to it that, after the mission, the agent who had surveyed the target with such attention to detail received the highest praise in his report. Glancing at his watch again, he found that only fifteen minutes had gone by. Releasing a silent sigh, he lowered himself into a cross-legged position on the ground. This was the only part of any mission that he hated. The waiting. It often gave one too much time to think of things that were not relevant to the operation. Things such as one's wife and children in Cuba who he had not seen for over a year now. Of the killing that would begin soon, and then, of course, there was the time to think of one's own death. No. The waiting was always the hardest part.

Across the street, the lights of both the first and second floors of the two-story mansion were aglow. Faint sounds of Spanish music filtered across the vast lawn and over the walls. In the ballroom, Miguel Duran, the governor of Lago Agrio, lifted his glass in a toast.

"Senoras and Senors: A toast to our honored guest, Senor Juan Garces, Minister of Finance."

"Saludar!" rang out around the room as the guests raised their glasses in a salute to the minister. Garces was a huge man who weighed over three hundred pounds. His bushy eyebrows arched slightly as he bowed to the group and he smiled while the glasses were raised in his honor—and rightly so. For he had brought good news for the rich and elite who now stood before him in this room. Lago Agrio's profits from the oil rich Northern Oriente region had doubled this year. The rich had become richer, thanks to his wise decisions and rather dubious manipulation of the country's finances. Indeed, they should be grateful to him.

The band struck up another lively Spanish song as couples made their way to the dance floor. Across the room, Paul Bracken, the U.S. consul general, stood talking with Colonel Robert Powers, Chief of the U.S. Military Advisory Group in Ecuador.

"Look at him. That fat son of a bitch is the biggest rip-off artist in the country and he's loving every minute of the attention," said Bracken.

"Yeah. But look at who he has for an audience. Only the richest damn people in this country. Garces isn't a fool. There are a lot of powerful people here tonight and he just wants to make sure they don't forget what he's done for them."

Bracken finished his drink and shook his head as he said, "You know, it amazes me how the people in this room can stand around drinking champagne and eating caviar, while over half the people in this country struggle to get by from day to day on whatever they can grow, steal, or dig out of a trash can. I'm telling you, colonel, if they don't start spreading the wealth from those oil fields to some of the poorer areas of this country instead of the major cities and their own personal bank accounts, they're going to have a full scale revolution on their hands."

"I agree, Mr. Bracken. But those fields have been pumping out that black gold for ten years now and the people who control the flow are happy with things just as they are. They're not about to change them, either. Hell, the under-the-table payoffs they make to the leaders of the military are so large that it guarantees them safety from military coups or takeovers of the old days. Right now they're sitting pretty and they know it."

Bracken took another drink as a waiter passed by.

"Yeah. Well, you mark my words, Colonel. This whole situation is going to jump up and bite them one of these days, and we're the ones who are going to have to treat the victims for rabies."

"Very uniquely put, Mr. Bracken," said Powers, as he smiled and nodded to Governor Duran and Minister Garces as they walked past the two Americans and out into the hallway.

Governor Duran kept his arm around Garces's shoulder as he led the minister upstairs to one of the bedrooms at the end of the hall.

"As always, my old friend, I have had your favorite room prepared for your visit," said Duran. Opening the door, he grinned as he patted Garces on the back and pointed to the bed.

"Both are Jivaro Indian girls; thirteen years old and virgins. Just as you like them. Enjoy yourself, my robust friend," said Duran as he closed the door and went back to the party.

Juan Garces's beady eyes were aglow in his heavily jowled face as he ran his fingers through grease-slicked hair. Wiping beads of sweat from around protruding, fat lips, he approached the bed and stared down at the two naked bodies lying before him. Their wrists and ankles had been tied to a specially designed bed. They lay spread-eagled on their backs, open to the lustful view of the giant before them. Long, flowing, black hair covered the pillows under their heads. The beauty of their bronze faces was obscured only by the tape across their mouths.

Moving to the small table beside the bed, Garces smiled broadly. His friend the governor had thought of everything. The frightened eyes of the young girls darted from side to side as they tried to watch the man's movements. A small laugh escaped him as he bent forward and picked out one of the six different sex toys that had been provided.

Tears streamed down their cheeks and terror filled their eyes as the fat man turned back toward them holding a thick, nine-inch vibrator, shaped in the form of a man's penis. With a smile born of pure evil, he flipped on the switch. The steady, loud humming of the vibrator filled the room as he knelt beside the bed.

Joaquin Ochoa allowed himself to drift into a light sleep. He and his men were going to need all their strength to complete this mission. Their target for the kidnapping was reported to weigh well over three hundred pounds.

Colonel Powers looked around the room, but couldn't find Paul Bracken. He was ready to leave and wanted to find out if the consul general would like a lift back to the hotel. Making his way out into the lobby of the main entrance, he spotted Bracken's aide, Mike Highfield. The stocky young man was a former Marine and now served as Bracken's unofficial aide and personal bodyguard. Moving across the lobby, Powers waved to get Highfield's attention. The two men met by the front door.

"Mike, where's your boss?" asked Powers.

Highfield pointed out to the balcony as he said, "He's out there with the foreign minister, Colonel. They wanted to talk in private; that's why I'm in here, instead of out there."

Powers fingered the curtain to one side. Both men seemed to be involved in a heated discussion. Paul Bracken was determined to make sure every member of the government knew where he stood on land reform and the mistreatment of the country's poor through graft and corruption. Powers considered joining them, but then decided he'd had one too many drinks to add any worthwhile comments to the argument. Releasing the curtain, he turned back to Highfield, who stood stone still, staring out the window at his boss. He had unbuttoned his dinner jacket to allow easy access to the Beretta automatic pistol that hung in a shoulder holster under his left arm. Being a bodyguard in any Latin American country was a risky business these days, but especially if you had a client who went around bad mouthing the host country's government officials and loved to drink when he did it.

"Well, Mike, looks like he's at it again. I'm going back to the hotel. Tell Paul he's welcome to fly back to Guayaquil with me in the morning. We'll be leaving about eight and we've got plenty of room. Have him give me a call."

Highfield's eyes never left the window as he replied, "Yes, sir. I'll let him know. Good night, sir."

Powers nodded, waving to his aide, Captain Mark Jackson, as he walked out onto the front steps of the mansion. Jackson joined him. While they waited for their car to be brought around, Jackson said, "Colonel, maybe it's none of my business, but since Paul Bracken is a friend of yours, I think you'd have a better chance of talking to him than anybody else."

"About what, Captain?"

"Well, sir, he's really starting to worry a lot of people in there. I mean—well, I can't be sure, but if I didn't know any better I'd swear I overheard some talk about getting rid of him."

"You mean, kicking him out of the country or 'rid of' in the more permanent form, like, no longer breathing? Which one, Captain?"

Jackson suddenly felt a little uncomfortable. He had only been in Ecuador one week and assigned as the colonel's aide only yesterday. To him, the kind of talk he'd heard going around inside was serious. Yet it didn't seem to faze the colonel.

As their car arrived at the steps, Powers turned to Jackson.

"Let me tell you something, Captain. This is your first tour of duty in a Latin country. Down here you're going to hear all kinds of threats, rumors, and talk of military overthrows. Most of them are just that: talk. I could name you six countries that talk about killing Paul Bracken on a daily basis."

"Why Mr. Bracken, sir?"

"Because he's goddamned honest, he can't be bought, and he really cares about the people of Latin America. That makes him a threat. So don't you worry about Mr. Bracken. He's been around a long time; he can take care of himself," said Powers, as he bent forward and stepped into the waiting limousine. Captain Jackson removed his hat and was about do the same when he suddenly stopped and stared across the top of the car, toward a dark corner of the west wall. He could make out a few trees and some of the hedges, but that was not what had caught his attention. He could have sworn he saw two figures drop from the top of the wall into the darkness of the trees.

"Any time you feel ready, Captain," said Powers in a sarcastic tone.

The young captain leaned into the car. He considered telling Powers what he had seen, or rather, what he thought he had seen. The look of impatience in Powers's eyes pushed the idea from Jackson's mind.

"What seems to be the problem, Captain?"

"No problem, sir. No problem at all," said the young captain, as he slid in next to the colonel and the car started down the winding driveway. They passed one of the security men walking along the edge of the drive as they neared the gate. "Damn," thought Jackson to himself. "It must have been the shadows of one of the security men I saw on the wall back there."

He hadn't even noticed the type of weapons the security people carried. Turning in his seat, he glanced out the back window to check out the man they had just passed. The security man wasn't there.

Joaquin Ochoa withdrew the blade from the man's throat and slowly eased the body to the ground. Removing a small transmitter from his pocket, he pressed the red button twice, signaling he had killed two of the security people. Within seconds, two more low beeps sounded over the transmitter. Two more men had been taken out along the west wall. That left only one more and Ochoa already had one of his men tracking the man down along the east wall. It would not take long. He sat in the bushes and waited.

Earlier, Ochoa had been awakened from his light sleep by the angry shouts of the commander of the guard. The commander's unexpected arrival had caught the gate sentries by surprise. There had been a lot of ass chewing and threats before the officer left. Utilizing the ravings of the officer as a cover, Ochoa hustled his team to the western edge of the woods. There they removed their silencers from the small black packs they carried and attached them to the ends of their MP-5 9mm submachine guns. Ochoa also removed an eight-inch suppressor and locked it in place at the end of his H &K P9S 9mm pistol. Signaling his men to remain in place, he maneuvered out of the woods, across the street, and to the west wall. Easing himself along the cool bricks, he moved to the corner guard post. One of the guards had been sleeping against the wall, next to the guard box. He placed the 9mm silenced pistol less than an inch from the man's temple and fired. Stepping over the body, he tapped on the wooden side of the box. The second guard came out and turned right into the barrel of the pistol. The bullet hit directly between the eyes. Ochoa grabbed the body before it fell and dragged it back inside the box. He then waved his men across.

Alfonso Robelo, the strongest of the five, braced himself with his back against the wall. Interlocking his fingers to form a stirrup, he nodded, as one after another, Ochoa and the remaining three men stepped forward and placed their foot in the stirrup and were hoisted up and onto the wall, then over and into the courtyard. Alfonso would remain hidden by the guard box for security. Once they had their target, they would use the west corner to escape.

Ochoa's transmitter beeped one time. All five security men had been eliminated. Fifty yards to the left rear of the mansion lay the security forces quarters. On the signal that the fifth guard had been killed the raiders were to regroup in front of those quarters. The three members of the team were waiting as Ochoa arrived at the position. No words were spoken; none were necessary. He signaled the men to spread out and pointed to the small house. Slowly and quietly the men converged on the front door. There was no light from inside. Ochoa felt the sweat soaking through the black mask that covered all but his eyes. Reaching cautiously for the doorknob, he secured a firm grip on the metal and began to turn it slowly. There was a slight click as the bolt cleared the doorframe. Ochoa stopped and listened to see if the noise had awakened anyone inside. There was only silence.

Ochoa eased the door open only enough to allow them room to slip through. Once inside, he quietly closed it again. They were in the living room. Allowing their eyes to adjust to the closed in darkness, they began to inch themselves along the walls to the hallway that lay only a few feet away. There were five closed doors along the hallway, two on each side and one at the very end. A small night-light in the bathroom cast a soft glow on the hall carpet. Ochoa and one man moved along the left side of the hall as the other two men took the right. Pointing to the doors to his right he nodded to his men. They acknowledged and each took up positions by a door. The man with Ochoa stopped at the first door. Joaquin shook his head from side to side and pointed to the second door. The man moved into his position while their leader moved on catlike feet to the door at the end of the hall. All eyes were on Ochoa. When he reached for the doorknob, so did the others. Raising the silenced MP-5, he stepped in front of the door. Turning to make sure everyone was ready, he nodded and kicked the door open. The man in the bed sat halfway up as he stared at the door through sleepy eyes. Eyes that saw only tiny flashes coming from the doorway. The phwfff-phwfff-phwfff sound of the silenced weapon on semiautomatic was not as loud as the heavy "thud" of the bullets as they impacted on the man's body, slamming him against the wall and over the side of the bed. Behind him, Ochoa could hear the deadly whispers of the other weapons as they claimed their victims.

Turning back up the hall, Joaquin saw the first door on

the left suddenly open and a naked man step out with a pistol in his hand. He turned and saw Ochoa. The sight of the man in black startled him for a split second. That was all the time Ochoa needed. Swinging the MP-5 up, and at the same moment thumbing the selector switch to full automatic, Joaquin unleashed the remaining twenty-five rounds of his magazine into the door, the man, and the wall.

Stepping over the mass of torn flesh that had been the naked man, he moved to the front window, pushed the curtain aside, and stared out at the mansion. Some of the lights on the first floor were going out. There was a line of arriving cars at the front of the house. The party was over. Ochoa studied the lighted rooms on the second floor. The man they were after would be in the last room on the south end of the hall. Removing a small black box from his shirt pocket, he opened it and assembled the syringe. Snapping his fingers, Joaquin waited as one of his men removed a small bottle from a foam-lined box and handed it to him. Turning the bottle upside down, Ochoa inserted the needle and drew the drug into the syringe. Passing the bottle back, he tapped the needle a few times and pressed the plunger in slightly. A small amount of the liquid shot out the end of the needle. Satisfied that all was in order, he returned the syringe to its box and placed it back in his shirt pocket. Looking out the window again, he saw that there were only a few cars left. They would wait fifteen more minutes before they made their move on the house.

Governor Duran bid the last of his guests good night and went back inside. The servants had already begun to clean up the mess left by Ecuador's elite. Looking up the staircase, he considered going up to see how his friend Juan was doing, but then decided against it. He personally found the man's sexual perversions distasteful, but one had to do what one must to maintain power, and the virginity of two Indian girls seemed a small price to pay to maintain that power. He just hoped the perverted bastard didn't kill them like he had the two last month.

"Hey! Where the fuck'd everybody go?"

Duran turned at the sound of the loud, irritating voice. It was Paul Bracken. The man was obviously drunk, barely managing to keep his balance as he leaned against the ballroom doorway.

"Where the hell'd all the rich shits go, gov?"

The governor's bodyguards came to his side and stared with loathing eyes at the drunken American.

"What would you like done with him, Your Excellency?"

"If I were to tell you the truth, we would be at war with the United States by tomorrow morning. The ravings of this drunken lunatic have caused me many problems. Take him upstairs to one of the guest rooms and dump him on the bed. What about his driver?"

The bodyguard replied, "He told him to leave hours ago, sir."

"What about that other fellow—the aide or whatever he is?"

Mike Highfield stepped from behind the ballroom doors. His dinner jacket was still open, and he had shifted the holster with the Beretta more to the front where everyone could see it. Taking Bracken by the arm, he spoke in a threatening tone.

"I'm right here. If there's any dumping going to be done around here, I'm the one that'll be doing it. Now do you think we could possibly borrow a car? I'd like to get Mr. Bracken back to the hotel."

Duran wondered if the man had heard his earlier remark.

"I wouldn't hear of it, mr.—Mr.—"

"Mr. Highfield!"

"Of course. By all means Mr. Highfield, please accept my offer of a room for the night. I'm afraid Mr. Bracken is in poor condition to travel the bumpy roads back to Lago Agrio. My home is his."

Highfield didn't care for Duran or his bodyguards, but he had a point. Paul Bracken was in pretty bad shape. "Which room?" asked Highfield.

"Top of the stairs, middle room on the right. I'll send one of my servants up right away," said the governor.

"Won't be necessary. I'll take care of him. It was a discussion about a country full of servants that got him in this condition."

Duran got the man's point as he watched Highfield wrap Bracken's arm around his neck and start leading him up the stairs. Halfway to the top of the stairs, Highfield stopped and turned to the three men standing below. "I wouldn't come around opening the door up here unless you knocked real loud."

Without waiting for any reply, he continued on up the stairs and to the room. Once inside, he locked the door and placed Bracken on the bed. Removing his 9mm Beretta, he checked to assure it had a round in the chamber, took it off safe, and placed it on the nightstand next to a chair. It was going to be a long night.

Ochoa watched the lights go out one by one along the first floor. All but two were out on the second. One in the middle and the target room. No matter, it was past midnight, they had to go now.

As they had done all night, the four men moved with ease through the shadows to a point below a balcony on the south end of the building. One man removed a long spike from his pack, folded out the seven-inch, barbed metal legs, and locked them in place. Another removed a nylon rope and attached it to the spike, then, moving the others back, he twirled the spike three times and tossed it up and over the balcony railing. Ochoa went first. Leaping up, he grabbed the rope and, going hand over hand, reached the top of the railing in a matter of seconds. The others followed.

The room off the balcony was shrouded in darkness. Slipping through the double doors, the group made their way across the sitting room and paused at a heavy oak door that led into the bedroom. A small ray of light could be seen spreading from the crack at the bottom of the door. Ochoa removed the syringe and slowly pressed down on the long, protruding, French-style handle on the door. He had thought of entering the room slowly, but changed his mind, deciding on speed and surprise instead. As the group rushed into the room, none were prepared for the sight that greeted them.

A disgusting slob of a man covered in sweat, with layers of fat overlapping in waves, stood naked by the bed, masturbating. On the bed before him were two young girls. One lay on her back. There was something protruding from between her legs. The sheet was covered in blood. The other lay on her stomach. She also had something sticking from between the childlike cheeks of her buttocks. A strange humming sound, as if a small generator were running, seemed to fill the room.

Juan Garces stared, dumbfounded, at the four men dressed in black as his hand continued to move. The fat man was beyond stopping himself now. It had taken him hours to get to this point. The raiders were equally shocked, if not more so, by the strange sight. Suddenly the realization of what had been happening in this room shot through Ochoa like a red-hot poker. Dropping the syringe to the floor, he sprang across the room and swung the butt of his rifle into the face of the fat man. There was a loud cracking sound as teeth shattered and bone broke in the man's jaw. He fell like a water buffalo. Ochoa's men gathered around him. Hatred fired their eyes.

"Untie the girls. See how they are."

Two of the men pulled their knives from their boots and moved toward the minister. Ochoa stopped them.

"I said the girls!" Reluctantly, they obeyed the order.

Garces began to come to. Blood ran freely from his shattered mouth and he moaned loudly. Ochoa dropped to one knee beside the quivering rolls of fat. Grabbing the white medical tape from the table, he reached down and snatched the fat man by the hair of the head and pulled him up into a sitting position. Peeling back the end of the tape he began to rap it roughly around the man's bleeding mouth. Tears flowed from Garces pain-filled eyes. After three firm wraps, Ochoa ripped the tape free from the roll. He could hear the broken bones of the man's jaw pop as he jerked the roll free.

Carlos Cruz, one of the raiders, knelt next to Ochoa.

"The little one on her back is—is dead, Joaquin. The other is hurt very badly. She has been beaten and raped. There is blood coming from her rectum. She can not live out the night without a doctor." Staring down at the repulsive animal that was Garces, Carlos asked, "Is this the man we were to bring back?"

Ochoa simply nodded. He was too filled with rage to speak.

"If our revolution shall depend on keeping animals like this alive, then we have no revolution," said Cruz sadly.

Joaquin Ochoa was a major in the Cuban Army. He had achieved that rank through hard work, obedience to orders, and successful completion of any mission he had ever been given. Tonight he was about to break those rules. Carlos was right. If the Ecuadorian Liberation Army had to preserve the likes of this scum to have an army, then they had no chance to begin with.

Joaquin looked hard into Cruz's eyes. He had made his decision. Nodding to the others to help him, they lifted the heavy man to his feet. The girls had been removed from the bed. Ochoa tossed the hunk of flab onto the bed and rolled him over onto his stomach while the others tied his wrists and ankles tightly spreadeagled. Across the room, Carlos held the injured girl tenderly in his arms as they both watched.

Giving each of the other men two of the various sized vibrators, he nodded at Garces. The first man stepped forward and ruthlessly shoved the smallest one between the man's buttocks and up his rectum. Garces's head shot up from the pillow in pain. Placing the second in the same place, the raider shoved the second one halfway in before it stopped. Stepping back, he opened the palm of his hand and swung it forward with all his might against the base of the vibrator. The object disappeared into Garces's body. Nodding to the next man, Ochoa watched as he tried to force this third one, only to have it stop less than halfway. Moving the man out of the way, Ochoa stepped forward and slammed the object all the way in with the butt of his rifle. Juan Garces's body shook as the first vibrator tore through the intestine deep within his stomach. Blood began to stream from his rectum as bile raced through his blood stream. It was going to be a slow, painful death. Tossing the other objects to the floor, Joaquin turned to Carlos. There were tears in the older man's eyes. The little girl had died in his arms.

Ochoa tried to think of what to do next. They had killed twelve men to get in here, only to kill the very man they were supposed to capture. All the work, the planning, and the risk had been for nothing. His superiors were not going to be interested in a story of two little girls and a depraved minister. He was ordered to bring back a very important man and instead, he had killed him. Now what was he going to do? His men would back him on his decision to kill Garces, but that only meant they would execute all five of them, not just him. There was always the governor, but he had his own personal bodyguards living right here in the house. They didn't know how many or where they stayed. Besides, they hadn't brought enough ammunition to take on a whole house full of people. Somewhere out in the hall a door shut. Carlos was standing by the door and waved for Ochoa.

Paul Bracken was feeling terrible as he tried to maneuver his way down the hall. He had awakened in a strange room, gone to the bathroom, and when he came out, he had walked right past the bed and into the hall. He hadn't even noticed Highfield asleep in the chair in the corner.

Carlos and Ochoa looked at each other. "What do you think, Carlos?"

Carlos raised his eyebrows slightly, "Hell, Joaquin. He looks important. A little drunk maybe, but important all the same."

Ochoa smiled for the first time that night. He didn't know who the man was, but the suit he wore cost more money than all five of them would ever see at one time. Somebody was better than nobody.

They waited until Bracken stumbled his way to their door. Ochoa opened it and he walked in.

"Hi ya, fellows. Say, you wouldn't happen to have a drink around would you? Heyyyy—nice outfits. Who's your tailor? James Bond?"

Bracken didn't feel the needle go in. Within seconds he was out cold. The raiders lowered him from the balcony and were across the yard and over the west wall by the time Mike Highfield woke up. He searched the entire house.

Garces's body was found, along with all ten of the security men and the two guards by the wall. The mansion was a madhouse as soldiers and bodyguards ran all over the place with weapons locked and loaded.

Back upstairs, Highfield picked up the telephone and waited for the operator to come on the line. Glancing out into the hallway, he saw the bloody, sheet-draped bodies of the two young girls being carried out.

"Number, please."

"The United States Embassy in Quito, please."

Highfield waited while the girl dialed the number. It was three in the morning. The line rang three times before the duty officer answered.

"U.S. Embassy. Captain Howlern, sir."

"This is Mike Highfield, CIA. Patch me through to the ambassador."

"Are you nuts? You know what time it is?"

Highfield was in no mood for any bullshit. "Hey, dick breath! Unless you wanta be answering phones in the septic tank of the world, you better make that fuckin' patch right now!"

There was a moment of silence on the line, followed by three rings.

"Hel—hello"

"Mister Ambassador. We've got a problem."

CHAPTER 3

B. J. Mattson turned the car off George Road and headed up the circle drive of the Rocky Point Golf and Country Club. It was 0645. Jake Mortimer lay back in the passenger seat, his eyes closed, his head pounding from a massive hangover. Mattson stopped in front of the clubhouse. A neatly dressed young man stepped from the curb and opened the car door for him. Jake moaned softly to himself as he forced open his bloodshot eyes.

"Are we there already?" he asked.

"Yeah. Come on, Navy, let's move it. When the ol' man says 0700, he means 0700," said Mattson as he handed the keys to the parking attendant and went up the steps of the clubhouse. Waiting at the door, he watched Jake trying to maneuver his way out of the front seat. It was a slow process.

They had both been on a roll by the time the club had closed last night, and were feeling no pain. The S-3 Air officer, Major Tibbets, had invited everyone to his quarters in an effort to keep the party going. Jake and B.J. had been just far enough in the bag to accept the major's offer. This had been a mistake. It was five in the morning when they left the party and B.J. got Mortimer to his quarters.

Mattson realized there was no way the Navy commander was going to get ready for their seven A.M. meeting by himself. He carried the bags up to Mortimer's room, then half dragged and half carried Jake upstairs and pushed him into an ice cold shower. While Jake called him everything from a whore to a mother fucker, B.J. busied himself with dumping Mortimer's clothes out on the floor and picking out some pants, a shirt, and some socks, laying them on the bed. He had had to wake the Navy man up twice. Once in the shower and again when Jake went to sleep bending over to put his socks on.

By 5:45 they arrived at Mattson's quarters. B.J. left Mortimer asleep in the car while he went in the house to shave, shower, and change clothes. His head was killing him too, but the thought of being late for the general's meeting provided a lot of motivation.

Walking into the bedroom, he found Charlotte asleep on the bed. She still had on the clothes she had been wearing the night before. On the nightstand next to the bed, sat a plastic drink cup half filled with Vodka and a book of matches with the name, "The Tropical Club," on the cover. He wanted to wake her up then. The problems in their marriage were getting out of hand. They needed to sit down and talk things out. But there hadn't been time. He let her sleep. Leaving, he quietly closed and locked the front door. Walking to the car, a thought crossed his mind. Maybe that was the problem. There never seemed to be any time. The matchbook, the Vodka glass, and the thought made the drive to the country club seem even longer.

"Come on, commander! Jesus, get you guys out of the water and you're slow as hell."

Jake moved his head upward faster than he intended. A pain ripped its way along his temple and shot through his eyes. "Screw you, Mattson," he mumbled as he stepped around B.J. and opened the door.

The two officers paused in the lobby, looking around for the general. Mortimer spotted a cotton-tufted head just beyond the rows of golf bags in the pro shop. Tapping B.J. on the arm, he said, "Five to one that's the man."

"No bet," replied Mattson, as he headed for the pro shop.

General Johnson turned and started up the stairs. Seeing the approaching officers, he looked at his watch. Waiting at the top of the stairs, he smiled as he extended his hand and said, "B.J., you're right on time as usual."

Even though the two men saw each other practically every day, the general pumped Mattson's hand as if they hadn't seen each other for years.

Jake didn't realize the general was such a large man. He had to be at least six foot two and a trim two hundred pounds. The bright yellow polo shirt he wore fit tightly across a broad, muscular chest. It was difficult for Jake to believe this body belonged to a fifty-nine-year-old man. The hair was the whitest white Jake had ever seen. It gave Johnson a certain look of distinction. It was easy to see where he got the nickname Q-Tip. The body had fared better than the face. It was a tough face, darkly tanned, with lines like cracked and worn leather scattered along the forehead and under the eyes. It was the face of a commander that had not spent a career giving orders to men from behind a desk, but rather one who led men into battle and shared their terror.

"This must be Lieutenant Commander Mortimer."

Jake averted his eyes from the mesmerizing white hair as the general reached out his hand. "Uh, yes, sir."

The General's grip was firm. "Heard a lot about you, son."

"I'm not sure if that's good or bad, sir," said Jake, smiling weakly.

"It was all good, Commander. Matter of fact, the Navy Department thinks very highly of you." Releasing his grip on Mortimer's hand, he continued, "Let's get some coffee, then maybe a little breakfast. What d'you say?"

"Sounds fine, General," said B.J.

Mortimer seemed to turn a little green at the mention of food but he nodded in agreement.

The general led them to a table in the far corner of the dining room, away from the main flow of traffic that was coming and going from the busy restaurant. As they sat down, a waitress brought over menus and poured coffee for all three, then departed.

"Well, Major. I'm glad to see you have better luck with Navy officers than you do with briefcases," laughed Johnson.

B.J. grinned as he reached for his coffee cup.

"I don't know, sir. I thought I'd lost him a couple of times last night."

Staring across the table at an ashen-faced Mortimer, Johnson said, "Had a chance to visit our fine officers' club, did we?"

Jake had started to answer but thought better of it. He still had a queasy stomach that teetered on the verge of nausea.

The waitress returned to take their orders. Johnson and Mattson ordered eggs. Jake passed. The very thought of putting something in his mouth that had dropped out of a chicken's ass almost gagged him on the spot.

"Well, Major. I suppose you and the commander here have a few questions about the purpose of this little get together, don't you?" said Johnson as he lit a cigar. The scent drifted across the table. Jake's face went green. In the battle of the wills, the stomach had won. Rising swiftly to his feet, he stood, weaving unsteadily for a moment, before managing to utter, "Ex—excuse—me, sir."

"Why of course, Commander. Feeling a little seasick, are we?"

Mortimer pivoted on his heel and walked rapidly across the room, breaking into a run only a few feet from the bathroom door.

"Good Lord, B.J.! What did you boys do to the Navy last night?"

"Oh, he was fine at the club, sir. I think it was the boilermaker contest we had over at Major Tibbets's quarters that did him in. I don't figure he'll die. Might be a little harder gettin' him in another contest."

"You better hope he doesn't die, Major. Otherwise, you'll be without a partner," said the general, as he tapped the end of his cigar on the ashtray in the center of the table.

"A partner?" replied a confused Major Mattson.

Johnson started to explain, but seeing Mortimer come out of the bathroom, he waited until the Navy officer was again seated at the table. Jake's eyes were wet and bloodshot, but other than that he looked as if he felt a lot better. General Johnson looked across the table at Mattson.

"Major, I believe you're aware of the problem we have within our headquarters."

"Major General Raymond Sweet," answered Mattson.

"Correct. The man is virtually chomping at the bit for a chance to nail us to the proverbial wall. He and that bunch of conventional twits that hung him around our necks can't wait for us to screw up an operation, so they'll have enough ammunition to get our unit disbanded."

Jake's trip to the porcelain goddess had helped. He still wasn't feeling great, but at least now he felt like he could talk without having to worry about messing up the general's yellow knit shirt.

"Excuse me, sir. The major has told me a little about this General Sweet. If he's such a pain in the ass, why don't you just dump him?"

"I certainly wish it was easy as that, Commander. Unfortunately, that is not the case. You see, General Sweet is the senior member of the Special Operations Advisory Board. A five man panel that reports directly to the joint chiefs of staff. They review our Special Ops planning for a certain crisis that may come up, then provide independent assessment and reviews to the joint chiefs."

"Excuse me, sir, but it is my understanding that this General Sweet is a conventional forces officer. How in the hell can he provide an assessment of an unconventional plan of operation? There is a hundred eighty degree difference between the two."

"Exactly, Commander. Therein lies the problem. Certain members of the joint chiefs, along with some nameless congressman, have intentionally placed an officer who is totally unfamiliar with and openly critical of unconventional tactics in one hell of a powerful position."

"Don't get the wrong idea, Jake," said Mattson. "Not all the members of the board are as hostile toward SOCOM as Sweet and the JCS. Admiral Charles of the Navy and General Howard of the Army are solid backers of the UW program. The Air Force and the Marines haven't made up their minds yet which side of the fence they want to be on. But it really doesn't matter. Even if all four of the board members approved an operation, Sweet, as the senior member, would have the power to veto it."

Mortimer shook his head as he said, "Damn, General, I thought we were all supposed to be on the same side."

"In a national crisis, we would be, Commander. But this is an in-house battle between the services and a few misguided politicians who have been convinced by our defense establishment enemies that Special Operations personnel are nothing short of a bunch of thugs with a Rambo mentality and a Charles Manson attitude toward life."

"It sounds like somebody at the Pentagon views SOCOM as a threat to their own organizations."

"You're right, Commander. And just what does one do when threatened?"

"Take action to remove the threat," answered Mortimer. General Jonathan Johnson nodded in agreement.

"That is why General Sweet has been assigned to SOCOM. In any situation requiring U.S. assistance, he has two main objectives: one, to assure that the Green Berets, the SEALS, the Rangers, along with our Special Operations wing, are given minor, low-profile targets to attack and then only in support of conventional forces; second, to exploit any and all mistakes made by our Special Operations people during any operation in which we are involved. Those mistakes will then be exaggerated to the limit by those opposed to SOCOM, followed immediately by an unexplained leak to the media. The more they can make us look bad in the public's eyes, the stronger their arguments to disband the unit."

Jake slumped back in his chair. "Jesus, I didn't realize there was this much back-stabbing going on within our own military. That kind of scenario makes SOCOM a sitting duck, General. In any operation there are bound to be mistakes and screw-ups, some worse than others. Hell, just look at what happened with operation Urgent Fury, the great Grenada invasion. The only damn thing that went right in that mess was the predawn drop of the Delta Force on Point Salines. After that, it was nothing but one major fuck-up after another."

The general looked up suddenly from his coffee cup. Jake detected a sadness in the older man's eyes as he softly said,

"There is no need to tell me about Urgent Fury, Commander. I was there from start to finish. I hope to God I never see another operation like that one in this lifetime." Johnson's voice suddenly broke. He paused a moment. Filled with emotion, he continued, "That is a perfect example of why SOCOM has to survive! We can not continue killing our young men through incompetence and petty bickering over who gets the glory! We—we just—"

The general's voice had risen to a level that had begun to attract the attention of other people in the dining room. Realizing this, Johnson stopped talking and turned to clear his throat. Jake thought he could detect tears welling up in the man's eyes. Johnson removed a handkerchief from his pocket and went through the motions of covering his mouth as he coughed again.

Mortimer glanced over at Mattson. That was no cough. The general was wiping tears from his eyes. B.J. moved his head slightly from side to side. Jake got the message: No more talk about Grenada. Johnson turned back to the table.

"Sorry about that, gentlemen. Beginning of a nasty cold, I'm afraid. Now, where were we? Oh, yes. Commander Mortimer, it may please you to know that you were selected for this assignment over all of your fellow officers within the Navy Special Warfare Group. You have quite an impressive record for a relatively new member of Special Operations. Your physical rating is superior. Academically, you are in the top two percent; you are highly intelligent, and through conversations with your superiors, I have been informed that you are a man who has no qualms about taking any action necessary to accomplish your mission. Would you say that is a fitting profile, Commander?"

Jake shifted in his chair and stared directly into Johnson's eyes. He replied, "General, sir, all modesty aside, I'd say that was a damn accurate description."

Johnson gave a short laugh as he rolled the cigar between his fingers and said, "They did mention something about your being very self-confident."

"Thank you, sir. But would you mind telling me just what I have been selected for?"

Mattson leaned forward now. The conversation so far had been interesting, but neither officer still knew why they were there.

"Surely. As I've said, we can not afford any mistakes. The life of this unit is riding on SOCOM performing flawless operations when called upon to do so. But as you yourself have said, mistakes are inevitable. There is always the unpredictable, and of course, Murphy's Law: If something can go wrong, it will. The President is aware of the dissension that has arisen from the formation of SOCOM. However, he cannot personally show favoritism one way or the other. I will tell you that, having spoken with him since the formation of SOCOM, he is a strong advocate of Special Operations. With my three stars, I have enough clout, shall we say, to handle any problems or interference that may arise during mission preparation. But once we have committed our people to an area of operation, I have to rely entirely on the team leaders on the ground. I have no way of knowing their every move or their every decision, whether right or wrong. A wrong decision on the part of any of these young officers can bring the organization down."

Mortimer felt a twinge of anger rise within him as he leaned forward, his voice tense. "Excuse me, sir! Are you questioning the ability of your own officers?"

Both Mattson and the general were surprised by Jake's question as well as the tone in which it has been presented.

"Not at all, Commander. SOCOM had the highest caliber of officers and professional soldiers of any military force in the world. But I am a realist, Commander Mortimer. There is no such thing as a flawless operation. I am simply stating a fact. As you said earlier, we are sitting ducks, and General Sweet is holding a shotgun to our heads. I do not intend to hand him the ammunition for that gun. Therefore, I plan to give SOCOM an edge. An edge against Sweet as well as Murphy's Law."

Johnson paused. Leaning back in his chair, he drew heavily on his cigar before looking at B.J.

"Major Mattson, you and commander Mortimer are going to be my eyes and ears on every important operation involving this unit. Sort of a combination of analyst, observer, advisor, and problem fixer, all rolled into a two-man team."

The two officers looked at each other with stunned expressions on their faces. Jake asked, "Sir, could you fine-tune that just a little bit more for us?"

"It's quite simple, Jake—it is Jake, isn't it?"

"Yes, sir."

"Fine. Well, Jake. Let's say some earth-shaking crisis occurs that requires the deployment of SOCOM personnel, say, the SEALS, SF, or Rangers. The White House alerts me. I, in turn, alert both of you. We identify the problem area, you and B.J. fly there, analyze the situation, make an evaluation of what assets will be required, then pass those requirements back here to me. I scramble the assets and have them on their way to your location within twenty-four hours. On their arrival in that country, you brief and update them on the situation. Now, I realize this seems like a hell of a load to place on only two men, but I firmly believe that working together, you can handle it. Jake, your selection for this job involved considerable time and extensive investigation. You adapt quickly to situations and it's well known that you prefer field work to staff bullshit. That's why you're here."

Smashing out the stub of his cigar before continuing, Johnson looked over at B.J.

"Major Mattson, you were my personal selection for the other half of this team for two reasons: One, you are a battle proven Special Forces medic with extensive combat experience. That alone makes you an asset to any team on the ground. Second, you are without a doubt one of the finest intelligence officers under my command. This has been proven by your work on missions in Central and South America. Your quick evaluation of the intelligence mission you conducted in South Yeman last year prevented another disaster similar to the Marine barracks incident in Beirut. Therefore, gentlemen, I feel that by having you along for the ride on these operations, SOCOM can narrow the odds for mistakes considerably."

Mattson and Mortimer sat back in their chairs and considered the full implications of the general's statement. They were, in effect, going to be his watchdogs over all major SOCOM operations. For Jake it was a welcome plan. All the worry about a desk and being stuck away somewhere in a staff job had been for nothing. He was going to be a key player in every mission that came down the pipe, loving every minute of it. For Mattson, it was not going to be that simple. He agreed with the concept and could see the advantages it would give them over Sweet and the pack of wolves that were after the unit's ass. He could see that; but Charlotte wasn't going too. This new job was not going to be as easy as the young Navy man sitting next to him thought. Hell, at this very minute there were forty-one conflicts taking place, involving forty-six of the world's one hundred sixty-five nations. They would be lucky if they had one weekend a month at home. No, Charlotte wasn't going to take the news very well. Not well at all.

Johnson noticed the concern on Mattson's face. "Something bothering you, Major?"

"Uh, no, sir. I only have a couple of questions."

"Fire away, B.J."

"Well, sir, once we make an evaluation and request, let's say a Ranger outfit for a raid type operation, who's going to be in charge of that operation?"

"The commander of the Ranger unit will maintain control. In effect, it is his operation. It is to be conducted by his people. You and Jake are there to offer advice. If, during the team commander's planning stage you foresee problem areas he has overlooked or failed to consider, you will tactfully get him off to the side and point these problem areas out to him. The same will be true once you are on the ground. The team commander will be in charge. At no time should the team feel that their commander has relinquished control of the operation to you. The only exception, of course, would be if the commander is wounded or killed. At that point you are to assume full control of the operation, reevaluate your position and make the decision to either continue or withdraw. I want you both to know that I have full confidence in any decisions you may make and that I will back you all the way, no matter what the outcome."

Jake wasn't exactly thrilled about not having full control over their operations, but it was a situation he could live with. Another thought occurred to him, as he asked, "Sir, what if General Sweet or some of his friends should begin to interfere with an operation? I mean, we're talking high-ranking officers and politicians with a hell of a lot of pull. They can throw a wrench in the works anywhere along the line."

A look of seriousness crossed Johnson's face. He knew the young Navy man was right. He found it ironic, no, pathetic was a better term. He commanded one of the most advanced, highly skilled forces in the world. A force that had to battle not only terrorists, Communist guerrillas, Cubans, Russians, and drugdealers, but attacks from people within their own government as well: a government that screamed for action against drugs and terrorists, yet continuously complained about the cost, delayed equipment requests, and placed roadblocks of every kind in the path of those who were supposed to do the job. Yes, pathetic was indeed a good term.

Johnson paused a moment to consider the ramifications of the answer he was about to give to Mortimer's question. SOCOM had tried to play by the rules, followed proper procedure, and bowed to authority in the hope that things would improve. They had not. Unfortunately, those attempts to appease had already cost the lives of more than thirty Special Operations people in the last year. They had been shoved into no-win situations with one hand tied behind their backs and the other held tightly in the grip of jealousy, greed, and politics. General Jonathan J. Johnson had had enough. If his people were going to have to die, they were going to do it with both hands free and swinging. Staring across at both men his voice was firm as he said, "B.J., Jake, for the record, should it ever become necessary, I and I alone, am authorizing you both to take whatever actions you may deem necessary to neutralize any interference, from whatever source, that may result in the failure of any mission being conducted by Special Operations Command personnel. And gentlemen: I mean any interference, from any source. Are we clear on that?"

Mattson and Mortimer looked at each other for a few seconds, then turned back to the general. Both replied, "Yes, sir."

"Very good then. Now, if there are no more questions, I suggest we enjoy our breakfast. Jake, you appear to be feeling better. Are you sure you wouldn't like something?"

"As a matter of fact, sir. I'm feeling a hundred percent better. I believe I will." Jake waved to the waitress and ordered. The conversation around the table had shifted from the previous seriousness to one of relaxed discussion about airline stewardesses and boilermaker parties.

CHAPTER 4

The general picked up the tab for breakfast, bid the two officers farewell, and linked up with his customary four-some for a round of golf. B.J. and Jake were on their way back to MacDill. Neither man commented on the general's directive on interference, although it was clearly on the minds of both officers. Ollie North had been given a personal directive somewhere along the line and look where he was now.

"Got anything planned for this afternoon?" asked B.J.

"I hope I'm going to get a tour of Tampa, courtesy of a long-legged redhead. Why? What'd you have in mind?"

"Thought maybe you'd like to come by the house this afternoon and have a few drinks. You could bring your date along if you like. Give Charlotte somebody to talk to."

"I appreciate that, B.J., but I think I'll pass. I've still got to unpack and try to get my stuff together. But I'd like a raincheck."

"No problem, Navy. The door's always open. By the way, something I've been meaning to ask you. Anybody ever give you flak about your name? I mean, Jesus, a SEAL called, Mortimer! The list of one liners and jokes that can be made from that one must be endless."

Jake took the question in the same good humor it had been asked. "Oh hell, yes. The full title is, Jacob Winfield Mortimer IV."

"The Fourth! Lordy, lordy!" said Mattson, with a laugh.

Jake switched his tone of voice and actions to demonstrate the proper blue-blooded upbringing of one raised in Philadelphia society. Placing his elbow in at his side, with his arm pointing up, he rolled his hand over and let it fall limp with one finger extended. "To answer your question, old boy, I have found that by articulating my full nomeclature in an establishment that disperses alcoholic spirits one can be assured of both an entertaining evening as well as an opportunity to demonstrate a variety of physical reflexes."

B.J. struggled to maintain a straight face as he looked over at his new partner and replied, "In other words, you want to start a fight, you just drop that moniker and see how many mothers you can kick the shit out of before they throw you out of the place, right?"

"Ya Fuckin' A!" shouted Jake.

Both officers were still laughing as they pulled up to the main gate at MacDill. The neat-looking AP with the well-pressed uniform waved at them frantically. As B.J. rolled down his window, the young sergeant bent down and looked into the car. "Sir, are you Major Robert J. Mattson?"

"Yes I am, Sergeant. What's the problem?"

"Is the gentleman with you Commander Jacob W. Mortimer IV?"

"Why, yes he is. Just wha—"

"Could I please see some identification? Both of you, please."

Jake and B.J. removed their ID cards and handed them to the guard, who studied them carefully, then went inside the guard shack and made a phone call.

"Wonder what's up," Jake said.

"You got me. You didn't make off with any of the dining room silverware, did you?"

The guard with the ID cards came back out to the car while another one rushed over to his patrol car, turned on his blue lights and pulled in front of the two men from SOCOM. Handing the cards back, the sergeant said, "Major, you and the commander are to report to General Sweet at SOCOM headquarters immediately. General Johnson is inbound by helicopter at this time. If you will keep up with our escort vehicle, we'll clear the road for you."

Without waiting for a reply, the AP turned and raced to the patrol car, the driver barely allowing him enough time to get all the way in the car, before he squealed his tires and flipped on the car's siren. B.J. stomped on the gas, burning rubber as he tried to catch up with the APs.

"I get the idea we're about to find out how well the general's plan is going to work."

"With the ol' man being picked up by helicopter at a civilian golf course, it couldn't be anything else. The only question is, where?"

They arrived at the Headquarters building in a matter of minutes. One of the two armed SOCOM guards posted at the entrance recognized Mattson. Both guards snapped to attention and saluted as the two officers passed them and entered the building. Major Tibetts, of boilermaker fame, met them in the lobby. His face seemed slightly flushed, as if he had been running.

"Jesus, am I glad to see you, B.J. That fuckin' Sweet has had everybody jumping through their ass around here. The ol' man's inbound right now. ETA in ten minutes." Suddenly realizing he hadn't even acknowledged Jake being in the same building, he reached out and shook the Navy man's hand. "How you doin' Jake?"

Mortimer nodded as Mattson asked, "What the hell's going on, Charlie?"

"About two hours ago we got a call from the White House. We got trouble down south. Somebody zeroed out the Ecuadorian minister of finance and snatched the U.S. consul general. They pulled it off right in the governor's mansion in Lago Agrio."

"Where in hell was security?" asked Jake.

"They found two soldiers outside the wall shot in the head, five of the security guys with their throats cut out on the lawn, and five more shot to pieces in their quarters. Whoever pulled this off knows his business."

"When did this happen?" asked B.J.

"Some time after one or two A.M. last night. Nobody is sure."

"How'd Sweet get in on this so fast? You should have notified the ol' man first, Charlie."

"Hell, B.J. You don't think I'd call that son of a bitch before I called the ol' man, do you? It was one of the new captains we just got in a few days ago. He'd just taken over as the officer of the day when the call came in. Being a new guy, I guess he got nervous. I mean hell, this was the White House on the line. He tried the General's home phone and when he couldn't get an answer, he got so uptight he forgot about the beeper call-up, so he called Sweet. Next thing you know everybody and his uncle is here running around like a bunch of chickens with their heads cut off."

"Did you get in touch with the general by beeper when you came in?"

"Didn't have to. Sweet told us where he was and where to send the chopper."

A surprised expression appeared on Mattson's face as he

looked over at Jake. How in the hell could Sweet have known that General Johnson was at the Rocky Point Golf Club? Only four people knew where they were supposed to meet. Outside of the three of them, only Sergeant Smith was aware of the time and place. And given Tommy's opinion of General Sweet, it was totally unlikely that he would tell the two-star anything. Johnson had entrusted the information for the meeting to Smith for only one reason. He trusted not only a sergeant, but a friend as well. No. There was only one way Sweet could have known where the general was. The ballsy little bastard had placed the commander of SOCOM under surveillance.

A squeaky, arrogant voice abruptly interrupted Mattson's thoughts.

"Well, Major Mattson, it's reassuring to know that you can take time from your busy night life to show some interest in your job," said Sweet as he crossed the lobby and joined the three men.

"Major Tibetts, do you have the schedules I asked for on the Quito airport?"

"Uh, no, sir. Not yet. I was just briefing, Maj—"

"Major, I would highly suggest that you at least attempt to achieve a higher degree of competence than normal and have those schedules on my desk in the next ten minutes. Is that understood, Major?"

Major Tibetts's face turned crimson. He would like nothing better than to bounce Sweet off the walls like a racquetball. Fighting to control the anger in his voice, he replied, "Yes, sir. Ten minutes, on your desk, sir." Spinning on his heels, Tibetts quick-stepped down the hall and into his office. The hallway echoed the sound of the slamming door.

For Mortimer, this was his first look at the man referred to as the albatross around SOCOM's neck. He reminded

Jake of Peter Lorre, a movie star from back in the late thirties and forties, who had made a lot of movies with Humphrey Bogart. Sweet was just as short, no more than five-feet-five. He had the same round build and squinty face with tiny, beady eyes and a few sprigs of black hair that had been spread to one side in a futile effort to hide a glaring bald spot. Sweet looked just the type of little rodent one would pick to play the role of Judas.

"Major, who is this man, and what is he doing here?"

"I'm surprised you don't know that already, sir."

"What?" barked Sweet in his shrill tone.

"This is Lieutenant Commander Jacob Mortimer, sir. He had been assigned to the command and just arrived this weekend."

Jake reached out his hand. Sweet ignored it as he said, "You'd be well advised to maintain a high standard of conduct in this command, Mortimer. An officer can never be sure of his next assignment, and a derogatory efficiency report can ruin a man's career. A point that many within this unit seem to have forgotten."

Mortimer tried to smile, but found it a major effort, as he said "I'll be sure to remember that, sir," then he asked, "Sir, did you command a unit in Vietnam?"

Sweet attempted to throw out what little chest he had, and replied, "Of course commander. Three tours and three commands. Why do you ask?"

"No special reason, sir. I just figured you must have had a lot to do with that war."

Raymond Sweet thought he detected a hint of sarcasm in the Navy man's tone, but let it go. Turning to Mattson, he said, "Major, I'm sure we have an extensive area study on Ecuador somewhere downstairs in that intelligence vault of yours. You will see to it that the information is in my office within the next twenty minutes. I realize that you are only the assistant intelligence officer, but Major Hatch has not arrived yet. Do you think you can handle that?"

B.J. bit his lower lip as he fought back the urge to tell Sweet to go fuck himself. The sawed-off little shit wouldn't know what to do with the information when he did get it. That was what he wanted to say, but he knew it would only create more problems for General Johnson, and right now they were going to have their hands full dealing with the Ecuador situation.

"Yes, sir. I believe I can take care of that. I could use Commander Mortimer's assistance, if that is all right with you."

Satisfied that he had made a lasting impression on the new arrival, and that Major Mattson was not going to be baited into an open argument, he waved them off. Answering Mattson's question as he walked away.

"Yes, yes. Whatever. But I want that information in twenty minutes."

"Real nice guy," whispered Jake as they watched Sweet go into his office.

B.J. laughed. "Oh, hell, yes. And just think, you met him on one of his better days. Come on, we'll go to my office and have some coffee."

"What about the area study?"

"Coffee first, then work. Coffee is the foundation of crisis management, Jake. Don't they teach you Navy guys that? Besides, nobody here does anything until the ol' man arrives. We just like to give Sweet the impression he's the big shit he thinks he is. Come on."

As the two men walked into Mattson's office, Jake asked, "You ever been to Ecuador?"

B.J. busied himself fixing the coffee as he answered, "Yeah, Last year, as a matter of fact. Didn't really get to see much. We were only in the embassy for a couple of days,

then headed on up to Colombia to do some work with the
drug enforcement boys. Only place I've seen where you can
wear short-sleeved shirts in the daytime, then have to switch
to a parka at night because it's so damn cold. You tell
people about zero degree weather and snow-capped volcanoes on the equator, and they look at you like you're nuts."

Mortimer sat in a chair next to Mattson's desk. While
B.J. fixed the coffee, Jake took the time to study the neatly
arranged office. A mahogany picture frame sat in the center
of the desk. It contained a picture of two children—a boy
and a girl—and a strikingly attractive woman. Under the
glass at one corner of the desk was another picture. This one
had been taken in Vietnam and showed two young soldiers,
barely out of their teens. One was Mattson. Dark shades of
camouflage covered their faces. Black gloves, with the
fingers cut out fit firmly over hands holding CAR-15
automatic rifles. Drive on rags, or Rambo rags, as they
called them now, were tied around their foreheads to keep
sweat from running down into their eyes. The two Americans in the picture were surrounded by eight similarly
outfitted Montagnard soldiers. In the background were two
rows of rucksacks, and beyond them the waiting UH1H
helicopters that were to insert the recon team. On the walls
were the usual plaques and framed certificates that marked
every soldier's assignments and accomplishments. One in
particular caught Jake's eyes. Rising from the chair, he
stood in front of the framed citation and read the details of
why Sergeant Robert J. Mattson had been awarded the
Silver Star for heroism in the Republic of Vietnam. Certain
words and phrases gave him an insight into the man
who was now his partner: "With complete and total disre-
gard for his own safety . . . single-handedly repelled a
counter-attack by two squads of NVA regulars. Although

severely wounded, and unable to walk, Sergeant Mattson, while under intense enemy fire, continued to move around the perimeter, administering medical treatment to the wounded."

Having finished reading the citation, Jake returned to his chair. Perhaps he had been too quick to judge those who he had considered losers of the Vietnam war. From what he had just read, Mattson had been anything but a loser. Yet, for every good soldier who had fought his heart out in Vietnam, there were an equal number like Sweet. Men with over-inflated egos that demanded others take notice of their importance, incompetent men, placed in positions of power that had done nothing more than give them the opportunity to step onto the world stage and openly display their ineptitude at war; and in the end they had lost. He wondered if B.J. ever thought about how it had all ended. One day he was going to have to ask him.

Pointing to the Silver Star award, Jake said, "That's an impressive narrative."

"Over-exaggerated," said B.J. "Actually, I was just trying to get out of there and all those damn NVA kept getting in my way."

"Modesty becomes you, Major," laughed Mortimer.

General Johnson stepped into the doorway. "B.J., Jake, in my office. Let's go." Both men jumped to their feet and fell in behind Sweet, Tibetts, and the rest of the staff as they hurried down the hall to Q-Tip's office. Once everyone was seated, Johnson took charge of the meeting.

"Gentlemen, I have just been on the phone with the President. The consul general is a close and personal friend of his. He and Mr. Bracken flew in the same squadron during World War Two. The President had only two questions: one, what would it take to get Paul Bracken back alive? And number two, how long would it take? I informed him that I could give him answers to both questions within the next twenty-four hours. I might add that at no time during our conversation was there any mention of negotiating or compromising with the people that have Bracken."

Johnson paused for a moment as Major Erin Hatch, the G-2 officer, entered the room with a stack of files under his arm.

"Good timing, Major. Gentlemen, Major Hatch will try and give us an idea of who was behind this incident and the latest intelligence from our embassy in Quito. Major, you have the floor."

Dumping the pile of folders on the corner of the general's desk, Major Hatch pulled a map from the cardboard tube he had been carrying under his other arm. Moving to a large map board behind the general's desk, he unrolled the huge map of Ecuador and tacked it to the wall.

"Gentlemen: Between the hours of twelve midnight and two A.M. this morning, a small unit of from four to six men made their way into the exclusive residential area of Lago Agrio." Hatch paused as he turned and removing a telescopic pointer from his shirt pocket, extended it, and placed the tip on an area in the upper northeast corner of the map, only a short distance from the border of Colombia.

"Their target was the home of his excellency, Miguel Duran, the provincial governor. A party in honor of the Ecuadorian finance minister, Senor Juan Melida Garces, was in progress at the time. In attendance at this affair were Colonel Robert Powers, Commander of the U.S. Military Advisory Group and his aide, Captain Mark Jackson. Also present were Paul Bracken, the consul general, and his personal bodyguard, a man listed as Mike Highfield. We know Mr. Highfield to be CIA. However, when I called the Agency this morning to get more information on him, they put me on hold for five minutes, then came back on the line and denied he had ever worked for them. Apparently,

Mr. Highfield has fallen from grace with the Agency and they are going to disown him after last night's kidnapping. He was there, after all, to provide security for the consul general, and they take it personally when they are made to look like asses. There were also approximately twenty-one other Americans present at this party, mainly oil executives and their wives or girlfriends. From a sweep of the area, conducted at first light this morning, they have found evidence that the team of kidnappers had taken up a secure position in the woods across from the main gate. Here they rested and waited until their plan called for them to go over the wall. Their intelligence as to the layout and schedule of activities around the governor's estate was exceptional."

Hatch paused and cleared his throat. Johnson reached across and poured the major a glass of water from a pitcher that sat on his desk. The room was silent and all eyes were on him as he took a sip from the glass and continued. "Thank you, sir. Now, early evaluation of the bodies found would suggest that the type of weapons used for this operation were 9 millimeter. Silencers must also have been used, due to the fact that no shots were heard, and yet no fewer than sixty rounds were fired in the security quarters prior to the snatch. This was definitely a well planned and executed operation, carried out by highly trained specialists. The number of people killed totaled thirteen. Two Ecuadorian soldiers, ten members of a private security firm, and the finance minister. Incidentally, you gentlemen may find the method in which Mr. Garces was killed to be particularly interesting. I will not go into detail, other than to say it was unique, and so far, we have no idea why this method was used. You will notice that in the list of personnel killed, not one American was harmed, although they were entering and exiting the estate all night. This certainly would have provided for a number of targets of opportunity, if indeed, Americans were the targets. Personally, I do not believe this team was after Americans."

Sweet had been sitting patiently through the briefing up to this point. Hatch's last statement provided an opportunity the antagonist could not pass up.

"That is a rather idiotic observation wouldn't you say, Major? Unless of course you are unaware of the fact that Mr. Bracken is an American."

Major Hatch seemed stunned by the sudden interruption, and completely lost his train of thought. Eyes in the room darted first to Sweet, then to General Johnson. If looks could kill, then Sweet would have been a dead man.

Johnson demonstrated remarkable control as he calmly said, "General Sweet, I would prefer that all questions or remarks be held until after the major has completed his briefing, if you don't mind."

Sweet could feel the tension around the room as the other officers stared at him. These Special Operations people obviously didn't take criticism very well.

"Of course, sir. If that is what you prefer. I just thought th—"

Q-Tip ignored Sweet's explanation. "Please continue, Major Hatch."

Hatch cleared his throat and fingered the pointer nervously. He had no desire to be caught in the middle of a feud between these two generals. However, Sweet did have a point.

"Sir, General Sweet may be right. As I said, my earlier statement was simply my own personal opinion and would seem to be flawed by the fact that Mr. Bracken was, in fact, the one kidnapped. Whether he was the main target for this operation, we have no way of knowing at this time."

A smug grin came over Sweet as he glanced at Mattson

and Mortimer. See, it hadn't been a stupid statement at all. Even the major said so.

Hatch continued, "The next question is, who engineered this operation? In Ecuador, we have four possibilities, although this, without a doubt, would be the biggest operation any of the four have attempted since they were established. These four are: The Socialist Party for Revolutionary Popular Action; several small Marxist parties united as the Communist Party, which follow the Moscow line; The Socialist Revolutionary Party, which follows the Havana line; and finally, The Broad Front of the Left. This outfit is made up of the extreme left and have united with the Maoist Popular Democratic Movement. The Communists exert considerable influence in labor, student, and intellectual circles. Of the four, it has been the Havana line group that has been most active over the past few years as far as military action goes. However, those actions have been limited to occasional destruction of power lines or small bridges, none of which have had any real effect on the country. The kidnapping of the consul general is a big step up for any of these groups. Colonel Powers, our milgroup commander down there has already begun organizing the Ecuadorian Armed Forces in case this is not an isolated incident. Security has been doubled at the embassy and the ambassador's residence. Similar precautions have been made for Ecuadorian officials as well. At present, we estimate there are approximately five thousand to seven thousand Americans in the country. These include military dependents, tourists and a variety of technicians and corporate executives. The United States has extensive financial interest in the area. You can be assured that the National Aeronautics and Space Administration will want to be kept informed of what's going on down there. They have a number of satellite tracking stations located in the mountains about thirty miles outside the capital of Quito." Major Hatch paused and turned to Johnson.

"Sir, that's all we've got for now. Colonel Powers will be sending intell updates every two hours from the embassy in Quito. He has dispatched his aide, Captain Jackson, to Lago Agrio to coordinate with the army unit in the area and to organize search parties."

"Thank you, Major," said Johnson as he stood and addressed his staff.

"Gentlemen, I would like for us to take a short break at this point and have some coffee. I want you to also consider our options and be prepared to make suggestions as to how we might deal with this situation. Major Mattson and Commander Mortimer, I would like for you to remain for a few moments. That is all, gentlemen."

The SOCOM staff left the room talking among themselves as they went into the hallway. General Sweet remained seated in the front row.

"General Sweet, there is no need for you to stay," said Johnson.

"Oh, that is quite all right, General. I've had my limit of coffee for the day."

"Then I would suggest that you make an exception and increase that limit today. I wish to speak to these two officers in private."

Sweet rose to his feet. He wondered what would happen if he refused to leave. Then, just as quickly, he let the idea go. He had to call the joint chiefs anyway. They would want to know what SOCOM was up to. Just as he reached the door, he paused and turned to face the three officers. "I'll remind you, General Johnson. I am merely attached to this unit. Appointed, I might add, by the joint chiefs. I am not one of your lackey staff to be ordered about like some shave-tail lieutenant!"

"I'll try to remember that, General," replied Johnson in a bored tone.

As the door slammed shut behind a frustrated Sweet, Johnson turned to Jake. "Well, Commander, I know you haven't had a chance to get your feet on the ground yet, but I hope you haven't unpacked your bags. B.J., I want you and Jake on your way to Ecuador in the next two hours. I'll have Major Tibetts make the arrangements. You'll have time for a quick run by your quarters to pick up what essentials you may need for the trip. I know this is short notice, but I have to know what's going on down there. The President is waiting for some answers, and the next time I talk to him I want to be sure they're the right ones. I want to know who, what, where, when, and how. Understood?"

"Yes, sir. What about the meeting?"

"Don't worry. It's not going to be anything but a smoke screen to keep Sweet off balance as to what we're really doing. We'll go through the whole business of planning a major operation just to keep him busy while you two find out what we really need to do. Figure you have seventy-two to ninety-six hours to get down there, scout out the situation, request assets, and bring this thing to a successful conclusion. It will take the other branches at least that long. Between alerting their units, trying to round up the equipment, and arguing among themselves, I'd say about that long. Four days, gentlemen. Don't waste them. I'll try to convince the President to stall as long as possible, but by the fourth day, the joint chiefs will be exerting all the pressure available on them to deploy a massive force to protect the lives of helpless Americans in the country. You can count on it. Now, get out of here, and good luck."

Both officers snapped to attention and saluted smartly.

"We won't let you down, sir." said B.J. as the two men left the room.

General Jonathan J. Johnson, stepped to the huge double windows behind his desk and stared out across the vastness of MacDill Air Force Base. He had just placed a thirty-year career and the future of SOCOM on the line. The establishment had left him little choice. He had to make them understand the importance of Special Operations. The days of the big battles and battlefields were gone. It was the era of the guerrilla fighter, the terrorist, and drug warlords. It was still a war, but a war that could not be fought with tanks and battleships. Those multimillion dollar weapons were useless in this type of war. The enemy no longer deployed his forces across vast battlefields with drawn battle lines. This new enemy lurked in jungle-covered mountain ranges, or among the civilian populace. He struck whenever and wherever he pleased, then just as quickly was gone. What good were tanks and eighteen-inch guns against such actions? No, massive firepower was not the answer. This enemy would have to be hunted down and destroyed in his own den. And J. J. Johnson knew he had the skilled hunters who could do the job.

At the far end of one of the runways, a Blackhawk helicopter lifted off. It gained altitude and swung out over the ocean. A moment of painful sadness gripped the white-haired man as he watched the bird until it was out of sight.

That was another reason he had to convince those in power of the effectiveness of Special Operations. Effectiveness that could be achieved only if SOCOM could control and conduct their operations without the interference of the other branches of the military. There could only be one signal caller in any game. More than that and you were courting disaster. SOCOM didn't give a damn about the glory that seemed so important to so many others. SOCOM only wanted to do the job it had been trained to do.

Turning from the window, he picked up the picture that sat at the corner of his desk and studied it for a long moment. There was a sense of pride in his eyes as he gazed at the eight-by-ten picture, but even that strong sense of pride could not overcome the emotions of a father. A small tear made its way down one cheek. In his hands he held the last picture taken of him and his son together.

Captain Larry J. Johnson, United States Army, had been a blackhawk pilot. His helicopter had been shot out of the sky by mistake in a place called Grenada.

CHAPTER 5

Peter Bracken had experienced his share of hangovers during his fifty-five years, but nothing to compare with the freight train roaring through his head right now. His mouth was dry as cotton and two attempts at opening his eyes had proved too painful. The glaring sun forced them closed.

Lowering his head, he felt something wet against his ear and suddenly realized he was lying on the ground. Where in hell was he? He had been on benders before and awakened in some strange places, but that had been in his younger days. As a matter of fact, there were still more than a few irate husbands out there who refused to believe that he had simply wandered into their wives' bedrooms and crawled in beside them by mistake. Once he had even awakened in a bed, naked, with a wife and her husband. He still wasn't sure of all the details of that one. One thing he was sure of, this wasn't some longhaired beauty's bed.

Somewhere in the background he heard voices. They were arguing, the words alternating between English and Spanish. Bracken felt something scurry across his face. Whatever it was, it had a lot of little legs. The shock brought his eyes wide open. He tried to sit up, but only made it halfway before falling back over on his side. His hands were tied behind his back. This was not right at all. What had he gotten himself into this time? Although he still couldn't focus his eyes, he could tell he was in a jungle by the sounds of the birds and the smell of mountain air mixed with the dead vegetation of a jungle floor.

Someone walked past him. He turned and tried to look up at whoever it was, but his vision was still blurred. There had to be more to his headache and lousy eyesight than an excess amount of rum and coke. What was the last thing he remembered before waking up?

Struggling to sort through the pounding blood cells racing through his head, he began to recall the night before in quick, picture-like glimpses. The governor's party—talking with Colonel Powers—the fat man, Garces—a sexy, inviting look from the banker's wife with the tight red dress and the big tits—an argument with somebody about rights—Highfield asleep in the chair—going to the bathroom—hallway, wrong door—black, something black. That was where it ended. He couldn't remember anything past that point. Hell, that didn't make any sense. He might be in a lot of places, but the Twilight Zone wasn't one of them.

The argument in the background had calmed considerably, with only an occasional, "son of a bitch" or "goddamnit" being emphasized. Someone stepped over his outstretched legs and began talking to another man in Spanish. Bracken squinted his bloodshot eyes a few times and stared at the boots that were only a few feet from his face. They were military issue jungle boots. Willing his eyes to remain open, he looked higher and saw camouflaged jungle pants tucked into the boot tops. Dangling just above the knee level, was the barrel of a rifle. Even with bad eyes and a hangover, Bracken knew a Russian AK-47 assault rifle when he saw one.

Lowering his weary head back to the damp ground, he

found himself silently praying that this was all just a bad dream and that any minute now an irate banker was going to storm into his wife's bedroom and wake him up.

Joaquin Ochoa raised his hands in frustration as he said, "But I have told you what I saw, what we all saw, when we entered that room, Coronel. You yourself have two hijas. I have known you since I was a boy of fifteen, Coronel. I know in my heart you would have done the same thing, had you been there."

Colonel Chato Suplao, the senior advisor to the Revolutionary Army, continued to pace back and forth between the trees, hands locked firmly behind his back. The anger in his deeply tanned face was highlighted by his coal black beard and mustache. The other members of the raiding party stood stone still at parade rest, just beyond the trees, as their leader, Ochoa, pleaded their case.

Stopping abruptly and spinning on his heel, Colonel Suplao pointed a finger at Ochoa.

"Do not try and play upon my sympathies, Major, by use of our friendship, nor that of my family. You fail to realize the seriousness of your actions. You allowed emotions, no matter how valid, to deter you from your primary mission. Not only did you fail in the mission, you also managed to complicate matters even further by abducting an American."

Suplao's voice increased in volume as he stepped closer to Ochoa and pointed down to Bracken's sleeping body.

"And this is not just any American, not a simple tourist, not a technician, not even a scientist!" Suplao was directly in Joaquin's face now. "But the Goddamn consul general."

Ochoa stood his ground, locking eyes onto those of his commander, as he continued to rave.

"We have spent over one year secretly training an army

of over three thousand men to infiltrate this country and lead
thousands more in an armed overthrow of this government,
a government so openly corrupt and cruelly standing with
its foot on the neck of the people, that the very mention of
the word revolution, brings us more recruits than we have
weapons for."

Ochoa did not have to search for words. They came
easily, and in a calm voice he replied, "I realize that,
Coronel. But if the fire of revolution truly burns so hot
within them, should the killing of one depraved minister
and the abduction of a single American official be enough to
extinguish that fire?"

Now it was Colonel Suplao's turn to throw his hands up
in frustration.

"Joaquin. Joaquin, my boy. You still do not understand
what I am trying to tell you. That single American, as you
call him, that man lying over there is Paul Bracken, the only
American in this entire country and possibly the whole
world that gives a damn about the people of this godfor-
saken place. He has openly condemned the government for
their attitudes toward the peasants on land reform, finance,
health care. My God, Joaquin. The man is practically a
saint among the very people we are encouraging to fight this
revolution. And now we, the Revolutionary Army, have
kidnapped the only honest man that would stand up and
speak out against their enemies. How do you think that will
make us look in the eyes of the people?"

Ochoa stood quietly, staring at the ground, a sinking
feeling in the pit of his stomach. It had been a major blunder
on his part. Not the killing of the pig, Garces, he would
never regret that, but the abduction of the American. That
had been his mistake. They should have withdrawn once the
objective ceased to exist. But the terrible sight they had
discovered in the room had pushed him beyond the limit.

Rage, not logic, had dictated the outcome of events. What was done was done. It could not be changed now. He was ready to accept his fate.

Carlos Cruz, the man who had held the dying girl in his arms the night before, stepped forward from the ranks of the commandos.

"Sir, may I speak?"

Ochoa's eyes came up and rested on the older man who had taught him many of the skills he now possessed. Colonel Suplao stopped his pacing and turned to the eldest member of Ochoa's team. An attitude of calm had returned to the colonel's voice as he answered, "Yes, Carlos, my old friend; of course."

"Coronel, this man, Bracken; he has not been harmed in any way, and I doubt very much that he is even aware of what has happened to him. Could we not simply return him to the outskirts of Lago Agrio? We have only had him for twelve hours. We could have him back before dark."

The beginnings of a smile pulled at the corners of Ochoa's mouth. Carlos was right. They had not harmed the man, other than adding slightly to a headache he would have had anyway.

Colonel Suplao raised his large bear paw of a hand to his chin and stroked his whiskers, as he considered the idea. No doubt the American government had already been alerted to the details of the kidnapping, and if they reacted in their typical fashion, then right now there was a room full of Presidential advisors suggesting everything from negotiating with the terrorists to calculating the overall effect of radiation fallout in a rainforest. At the same time in another room generals would be figuring how many battleships, aircraft carriers, and submarines they could move into position along the Ecuadorian coast. Within a matter of seventy-two hours they will have divided up the country on a map and paratroopers would be falling from the sky like rain. The very thought of that brought a sudden outbreak of sweat to Suplao's brow.

This was not working out to be the well kept secret infiltration and preparation for a revolution that had been envisioned by Fidel and his advisors. So far only five hundred of the three thousand guerrillas had been infiltrated into the mountains around Lago Agrio. Another five hundred were due to arrive off the coast of Valdez tomorrow night. The remaining two thousand were still at the training camps at Ostional and Tamagas in Nicaragua. They, too, were to be infiltrated into the country over the next two weeks. Over a year of planning and training had gone into this operation and now it all hinged on Suplao's decision of the next few minutes.

There was perfect silence from those who stared at Suplao. In one way or another they fully understood the pressure that had been placed on their commander. Ochoa most of all, understood Suplao's predicament.

Removing his hand from his chin and rubbing the tense muscles in his neck, Suplao carefully sorted through the possibilities. If Bracken suddenly reappeared unharmed, then there would be no need for a vast deployment of American soldiers into Ecuador. The man had been out cold ever since being abducted. He had not seen any of his captors, nor where he had been taken; therefore he could give no damaging information that could possibly compromise their identity or location. Another shot of the drug to assure he did not wake up would enable them to move him to a place near the town where a search party was sure to find him. Of course the Ecuadorian Army would continue to search for the killers of the finance minister, but not with the same intensity they were surely using to find the American. It was too late to halt the arrival of the five hundred men due in tomorrow night. Perhaps the safe return of Bracken by tonight would diminish the number of patrols along the coast. He would have to radio for an additional two week delay for the arrival of any more troops from Nicaragua. By then things should have returned to normal. The initial plan would remain intact and he would receive only a verbal reprimand for the delay, while Ochoa would be spared a bullet in the head. Turning to Ochoa, he asked, "Do you still have the needle and the drug?"

Ochoa breathed a sigh of relief as he pointed to Carlos. The old man already had the bottle and the black box held high in his hands, a smile beaming across his lined and weather worn face, as he yelled joyfully, "Si, si, mi Coronel."

"Well, hurry up then. We must make sure that Senor Bracken is found before nightfall."

Suplao had warned Ochoa that getting the American back would be ten times harder than getting him out had been. He had not exaggerated. The trip down from the mountains had been no problem, but the closer they came to the valley of Lago Agrio, the more patrols they encountered. So far they had evaded three army patrols and two helicopter flyovers and they were still ten miles from the outskirts of the town.

A litter for Bracken had been formed from two long branches, strips of tree bark, and the few nylon ponchos they had. The consul general had stirred for a moment when given the drug, but now as the litter was maneuvered down the mountainside, Paul Bracken slept like a baby.

Counting Ochoa, the squad picked for the return numbered ten. Each of the search parties they had so far encountered had outnumbered them three to one. A few of the younger guerrillas demonstrated their inexperience by displaying an overzealous desire to take on the fully equipped government troops in an open confrontation. Ochoa had found it necessary to slap one of the more vocal hotheads in this group. That had put an end to the discussion. The last thing in the world Ochoa wanted now was a firefight with anybody. One stray bullet or a grenade and Bracken could be killed. Then what would he do? Joaquin didn't even want to think about it. He had already bungled the first mission; he had no intention of allowing that to happen again.

Another five miles and two hours later he halted his small team for a rest break. They had not crossed paths with any more patrols and had only heard the choppers in the far distance. One of the young guerrillas had asked why they had not simply left the American where they had spotted the first government troops? Ochoa had gave him two reasons; one, the troops had been going away from them, not coming toward them. The closer to the town the better the opportunity to find a clearing or road that would guarantee he would be found. Second, the reason they had made a wide circle to the east side of the town was to assure that no trails or line of march could be traced directly back to their mountain base camp.

Small streams of perspiration made their way down Ochoa's cheeks as he pulled a map from the side pocket of his jungle fatigues. Carlos Cruz came over and sat down beside him. "How much farther, do you think?" he asked.

Ochoa glanced around at the terrain then pointed to a small group of ridgelines on the map, just beyond the valley of Lago Agrio. "We are here. There is a main road less than one mile from the edge of the valley, often well traveled. That would be a good place."

"The men will be glad to be done with this business. Many are becoming nervous because of the helicopters," said Cruz wearily.

"Believe me, Carlos, my old friend, they could not possibly want this thing over with any more than I do. Tell them we will move again in five minutes." Ochoa shook his head.

Carlos rose to his feet. "I will let them kno—" Cruz stopped in mid-sentence and suddenly dropped straight to the ground and pointed in the direction of the hill they had just come down. Instinct, brought on by the sudden move of Cruz, sent Ochoa and the others flat to the ground, their eyes staring up the hillside.

Twenty-five to thirty Ecuadorian soldiers were moving on line down the side of the hill. They had not spotted the guerrillas yet, but it was only a matter of time. They were too spread out to possibly miss Ochoa and his group. Looking over his shoulder, Joaquin saw his men pressed close to the ground, their weapons pointing up the hillside. Bracken and the litter lay in the open. There was no time to move him now. No time for them to escape. They had lost the advantage of the thick jungle cover midway down the hill. There was only knee-high grass and a scattering of trees. Any attempt to run away now would expose them all to the soldiers on the hillside. Praying a silent prayer to all the saints he could think of, Ochoa slowly brought his rifle up and into the firing position.

The soldiers were less than fifty yards away now and still on line. Some had their rifles over their shoulders; others carried them loosely in one hand at their side. As with the guards at the governor's mansion, these soldiers had quickly become bored with the search and obviously did not expect to find anything or anyone this close to the town. It was this relaxed attitude that gave Ochoa and his men the break they so desperately needed.

One of the soldiers to the far right of the line was staring up at the sky when his boot suddenly caught on a tree root and sent him pitching forward, head over heels. He rolled a couple of times, then slammed full force into a tree trunk. A loud cracking sound was quickly followed by a scream that echoed down the hillside. The line stopped as the soldiers rapidly brought their weapons to the ready position, uncertain of what had happened. The soldier with the broken leg screamed again more loudly. Cries for help came from those closest to him. The well organized line of only moments before deteriorated to no more than a mob as all the soldiers gathered to the right to see what had happened.

Ochoa glanced at Cruz and winked. Their prayers had been answered. Looking back at the others, he signaled for them to low crawl off to their left. Remaining pressed to the ground, the squad obeyed and began the slow silent maneuver. In a way this had worked out perfectly. The army commander would now have to call in a medievac for the injured soldier. In the meantime they would find Bracken and could put him on the same bird. Finally something had worked out right.

Nodding to Cruz, both men slid slowly backward on their stomachs, eyes riveted on the men along the hillside. Slowly turning to their left, they began to inch themselves closer to the thick jungle cover just beyond the trees. They were nearly out of sight when Ochoa heard a sound that sent a chill down the back of his neck. It was the heavy thudding sound of a bolt going forward. Looking to his right, he saw the young loudmouth he had backhanded earlier on his feet, his AK-47 pressed against his hip and pointed at the soldiers. As the young fool began to run toward the soldiers he screamed out in a loud and clear voice, "Bastardos!" He followed the insult with a long burst of automatic fire from the AK-47. The sound of thirty rounds of 7.62 lead thundered along the hillside.

"No!" yelled Ochoa, as he leaped to his feet and looked

up the hill. Chunks of dirt and puffs of dust danced among the crowd of startled soldiers as they stared in shock at the lone gunman charging up the hill at them. It wasn't until two of the bullets found their mark and ripped through one soldier's chest, splattering the others with blood, that they reacted. Some dived for cover while others fell to the prone position and opened up full automatic at the darting and weaving figure of the madman who continued to run at them while changing magazines in his rifle.

Cruz, on his feet and grabbing Ochoa by the arm, yelled, "Come, Joaquin! You can do nothing for him. The young fool has killed himself."

It wasn't the fool that concerned Ochoa. It was the sight of the dirt and leaves leaping from the impact of the soldiers' bullets as they hit all around Bracken and the litter. He was supposed to have been returned unharmed. Now, ironically, the very soldiers who had been sent to search for him could be the ones who killed him. Carlos forcibly pulled Joaquin into the jungle cover to the left, just as bullets began to hit in the trees above their heads. The last thing Ochoa saw as he disappeared into the jungle was the body of the young guerrilla, engulfed in a hail of lead, dirt, and dust as it was torn to pieces by the concentrated fire of the soldiers on the hillside.

The soldiers continued to fire into the lifeless body for a full minute, some out of fear, others out of anger. Juan Sanchez, the young captain in charge of the army unit, finally screamed for a cease fire. Waving for his troops to spread out, they again moved forward, this time with alert caution. There was no need for it now. Ochoa and his squad were already out of the area and on their way back to the mountain base camp. Slowly, they gathered around the ripped and torn body. There was no way to tell the age of the guerrilla. The face and most of the head had been shot away, the uniform was nothing more than blood-soaked, tattered rags. The wooden stock of the AK-47 lying near the body had been shot into splintered pieces of wood.

From beyond the crowd of soldiers someone yelled out that they had found another man. Captain Sanchez pushed his way through the crowd and rushed to where a soldier stood over a man on a litter. He recognized the American immediately. A wide smile came over his young face. He, Captain Juan Sanchez, had found the missing consul general. Visions of promotion and glory danced in his eyes. Not only had he rescued Paul Bracken, but he had also fought a battle against the guerrillas. Of course there had only been one guerrilla, but then again, who was to say there hadn't been, say, thirty or forty more, firing at them from the jungle to the left? In all the excitement, noise, and confusion, who could tell how many guerrillas there had been? Better yet, who among his troops would dare question their commander? A soldier with a radio on his back approached him. Headquarters was on the line. It was Colonel Rivas, the battalion commander. Sanchez pressed the talk button. His voice displayed a certain cockiness as he said, "Mi Coronel, we have just fought an engagement with a heavily armed force of Communist guerrillas only five miles from the town."

"What are your casualties?" asked the colonel.

"One man killed. Two men wounded. We will require a medievac helicopter."

"How many Communists were killed?"

Sanchez paused a moment. He could fabricate the numbers, but not the actual bodies that they would surely want recovered. Then he remembered the stories he had heard of Vietnam.

"Unfortunately, we were only able to recover one body, Coronel. The guerrillas exerted very heavy firepower to keep us pinned down while they dragged away the ten to fifteen others. But there are many blood trails leading away from the battle site."

A few of the soldiers standing near Sanchez began looking around on the ground as if actually expecting to find the blood that had been mentioned. An old NCO with the group shook his head sadly then tapped the captain's arm. "Do not forget the news of the Americano, mi Capitan."

Sanchez had become so involved in his own battle exploits that he had totally forgotten about the American.

"Coronel, you will also be pleased to know that we have rescued the American consul general."

There was a long pause on the colonel's end of the line.

"Coronel, did you hear what I said? We have found Senor Bracken."

"Is he all right?" asked Rivas.

"Si, mi jefe."

Colonel Rivas asked for their position and told Sanchez to prepare a landing zone. Helicopters would be sent to extract them all at the same time, and return them to the army compound outside the city. Rivas congratulated them on a job well done as he signed off.

Captain Sanchez was in exceptional spirits as he and his men waited in the clearing just east of the hill. They could hear the helicopters coming up the valley. He would be promoted at least to major for his actions today. The press, of course, would want the details of his heroic battle against the Communist guerrillas. His picture would be on the television and in all the papers. He was going to be famous, a hero.

The whopping sounds of chopper blades became louder as they swooped over the hill to the site of the soon-to-be-famous battle, and passed over the clearing. Sanchez got his men to their feet and ordered his sergeants to break the men down into loading order. Shading his eyes against the afternoon sun, he stared up at the helicopters. There were five, UH1H Huey helicopters making a wide circle to the left. Squinting his eyes, Sanchez could see the bright yellow, blue, and red stripes, the national colors, on the door of the lead chopper. That was Colonel Rivas's personal helicopter. This indeed was an honor. Perhaps he was to be promoted on the spot.

As the colonel's helicopter landed Sanchez ran the short distance to the side door and met Rivas as he stepped out. A side door slid open and two medics dashed to where Bracken lay on the stretcher.

"A fine job, Captain," said Rivas, as he shook the excited young officer's hand. "We will see that both you and your brave men are rewarded for your actions today."

The two medics carried Bracken to the colonel's helicopter as Sanchez said, "Gracias, mi Coronel."

Pointing up at the four remaining choppers that were still circling above them, Rivas said, "Those helicopters are for you and your men, Captain. I must get Senor Bracken back immediately. I'm afraid there is little room left in my helicopter; otherwise I would be honored to have you ride with me. I hope you understand."

"Of course, Coronel. It is better that I stay with my men. I shall see you back at the headquarters."

The two men shook hands again. Rivas climbed back aboard his chopper, smiling and waving as the bird lifted off. Captain Sanchez ran back and checked to be sure his men were in the proper order to board the incoming choppers. The size of the clearing provided more than enough room to allow all four of the helicopters to land. They came in, one behind the other, and hovered a few feet off the ground.

Unable to make himself heard above the deafening noise generated by the whirling blades, Sanchez raised his arm and signaled for his men to board. Bending his head slightly, and putting a hand in front of his face to shield his eyes from the swirling grass and dirt blown about by the down draft of the rotors, he began to move forward. Suddenly he felt a stinging sensation along the side of his right leg. Then another, more painful one, along his left side. Turning his head to the left, he saw his men grabbing at their chests and stomachs. What was happening? Looking up at the choppers, he received his answer. The steady red-orange flashes of the door mounted M-60 machine guns spat death from all four helicopters. A bullet tore through his arm, spinning him around in time to catch two more slugs in the middle of his back, the impact from the 7.62 rounds slamming him to the ground. The slaughter had taken less than a minute. To be sure, the choppers rose twenty feet and hovered once more, providing a better angle for the door gunners to rake the bodies one last time, before leaving.

Another bullet struck Captain Sanchez in the left shoulder blade, shattering the bones, the impact flipping the man over on his back. It hadn't been necessary. The captain was beyond feeling any more pain. The reflections of the departing helicopters were mirrored in Sanchez's lifeless eyes as they passed over the bullet riddled body of the man who would be a hero.

CHAPTER 6

Jake Mortimer stared out the window of the Lear jet as they passed over the snow-capped peaks of the area known as the Avenue of Volcanoes.

"Man, that's really something. Snow-topped mountains with jungle rainforest on both sides, one freezing, the other hotter than hell. It seems kind of unnatural in a way. Don't you think, B.J.?"

"Yeah. That's the same thing I thought, the first time we flew in here. You see that big one over there? That's Chimborazo; twenty thousand five hundred feet above sea level." Pointing to some others farther to the north, B.J. said, "The smaller of the two you see over there is San Antonio de Pichincha. It's only seven thousand feet high, but you know where you'd be if you were standing on that baby?"

"Give me a break, Mattson. After all, I am a Navy Officer, you know. That must be where the longitude and latitudes cross the equator, right?"

"That's very good, Harvard. On a navigational chart you'd be standing at zero degrees, zero minutes, and zero seconds."

Jake sat back in his seat as he laughed and said, "That

must be why all you army guys know that one. It's easy for you to find on a map."

Mattson was searching for a come-back when a soft bell toned and the fasten seat belt sign came on above the pilot's cabin. Looking out the window again he could see they were approaching the outskirts of Quito, the capital and the oldest city in Ecuador. In the background stood Cotopaxi, the city's snow-mantled overlord. The still active volcano, towered nearly two miles above a capital that had survived eruptions, earthquakes, and conquest by both the Inca and the Spaniards.

B.J. looked at his watch. It was mid-afternoon. The had made good time. Colonel Powers had been informed of their arrival and would be waiting with transportation to take them to the embassy. As he sat back, listening to the hum of the hydraulics as the landing gear was lowered, Jake asked, "How did the little lady take the news of your sudden, unexpected vacation?"

Mattson lied. "It didn't surprise her much. She's kind of grown used to it by now. Told me to have a good time, but to stay out of the whore houses."

Jake smiled, then relaxed in his seat and closed his eyes. Mattson wasn't smiling. There was nothing to smile about. He didn't think anybody could have a good time in hell. That was where Charlotte had told him he could go when he had walked out the door this morning. He had only had thirty minutes to throw some things together. Twenty-five of those had been spent in a yelling contest with her. She had wanted to know where he was going. He couldn't tell her. When would he be back? He didn't know. They had to talk. He couldn't. There wasn't any time left. For once she had agreed with him. B. J. Mattson had a feeling she wasn't going to be there when this was over.

As the pilot made his final approach, they passed over the

open air markets of the squares that were surrounded by long, low, broad-eaved houses with faded, red-tiled roofs, and glided smoothly onto the runway. They slowed and taxied off the main strip to a hangar area reserved for VIP arrivals. Staring out his window, Mattson spotted the three embassy cars along the fence next to the hangar. Security was heavy around the vehicles and soldiers were spread every twenty feet along the chain link fence that encompassed the small area. Their weapons were not slung, but rather held in the ready position, as if at any minute they expected to come under fire from somewhere.

"I would say those boys are taking this business pretty serious," said Jake.

"No shit!" replied Mattson.

The small aircraft swung around near the gate and stopped. The side door was opened and the steps lowered. The two SOCOM specialists stepped out into the afternoon sun. They wore civilian clothes and Jake was already wishing he had taken B.J.'s advice and worn a long-sleeved shirt. Even through the sun was still up, there was a nipping chill in the wind.

A tall, husky man in his late forties and two younger men in their twenties came through the gate by the cars and walked toward the plane. The older man reached out a large hand that seemed to have exceptionally long fingers and said, "Major Mattson. Commander Mortimer. I am Colonel Robert Powers, and these two gentlemen are Sergeant Larry Rivers and Sergeant David Maloy, Marine security from the embassy."

Handshakes were exchanged all around. "Do you gentlemen have any luggage that needs to be unloaded?" asked Maloy.

B.J. held up a canvas athletic bag. Jake had one too. "No, Sergeant. We're traveling light on this trip."

"That's fine," said Powers. "Now, if you will follow me, we'll be on our way."

The colonel led the way as the three officers went through the gate and stepped into the middle car.

"Are we ready, sir?" asked Maloy.

"Yes. We're clear, sergeant. Let's move it out."

Sergeant Maloy ran up to the lead vehicle and slid in beside the driver. Two more security people suddenly appeared from somewhere beyond the fence and climbed into the tail vehicle with Sergeant Rivers.

The driver flipped his lights on and off once. The lead car pulled out, followed by Powers and the rear security, all three drivers making sure that there was never more than one car length between each of the vehicles. Observing the tight security being taken, B.J. said, "It would appear, Colonel, that the level of excitement in this country has heated up since we departed from MacDill this morning."

Colonel Powers leaned forward. Resting his arms on his knees, he interlocked his long fingers as he answered, "You might say that, Major. While you have been in the air for the last five hours, business has picked up considerably. About three hours ago, an army search team of thirty men were ambushed and wiped out only six miles from the town of Lago Agrio. There were no survivors. Less than two hours ago in Guayaquil, the country's second largest city, two American executives from the Bendix Corporation were gunned down one block from the U.S. Consulate building. Nailed them both with automatic weapons from a speeding car. And as if that wasn't enough for one day's work, the bastards called and politely informed us that the embassy would be next and that any American in the country, regardless of their status or position, would be considered a target. So yeah. I'd say it's picked up a bit."

B.J. looked over at Jake. No words were necessary.

Reaching into their travel bags, both men removed 9mm Berettas and shoulder holsters. Shifting around in the spacious back seat, they slipped into the rigs, checked their magazines, then loaded the weapons, made sure the safeties were on, and snapped them in the holsters. Powers watched the action in silence. After what he had just told them, it would be a little ridiculous to assure them they were safe for the moment.

"We have any idea exactly who 'they' are?" asked Jake.

"That seems to be the million dollar question, Commander. It depends on who you want to talk to. My people have keyed in on the Mao Movement. They've been preaching some hard-line militant rhetoric in their last two political rallies. Standard stuff, you know: 'The hour of the people is near. Action shall speak louder than words,' all the usual Commie bullshit."

"What about the Agency boys?" asked Mattson.

"Well, at first they pinned it on a radical group that had split off from the Democratic Left. Then, with the report of the army wipeout, they switched it to the Revolutionary Popular Action Group. That didn't last long either. When the Bendix guys bought it the Agency swore it had to be the Carlos Medineo faction of the FADI, an extreme left group that's been involved in a number of shoot-outs with the local police. Like I said, it just depends on who you're talking to at the moment."

"What's your opinion, Colonel?" asked Mattson, scowling.

"You want the truth?"

"Absolutely," said B.J.

The colonel shook his head. "Major, nobody has any fucking idea!"

Mattson and Mortimer leaned back in the seat. This wasn't going to be as easy as they had hoped.

• • •

General Arturo Jose Parros and Colonel Ernesto Rivas ignored the salutes of the guards as they walked up the steps and through the doors of the governor's mansion. Miguel Duran was coming down the spiral staircase, followed by an entourage of bodyguards, as the two officers entered. The general's tone of voice toward one that was supposedly his superior, was far from gracious.

"Governor Duran. This is the second time I have had to come here today. I am a very busy man. This had better be important."

Although the mansion was equipped with central air conditioning, Duran was sweating heavily. The general's sharpness only added to the official's nervousness.

"It—it is important, General. Come, we can talk in my study."

Allowing the two military men to enter first, Duran informed his chief bodyguard that they were not to be disturbed. Closing the heavy oak doors of the study behind him, Duran crossed the room and went behind the bar. Pulling a bottle of tequila from the cabinet, he poured three glasses and offered them to the officers. Parros stared at Duran with his cold dark eyes.

"Duran. I am a busy man. You drink if you must—and from your appearance I would say that you are a man in desperate need. Now, why have you bothered me again? You know that Colonel Rivas and I have much to do before nightfall. Well, come man. I haven't all day to stand here and watch you suck down your courage."

Duran's hand was visibly shaking as he raised the glass to his lips, spilling a small amount on his white silk shirt. God, how had he let himself be talked into this insanity? True, with the death of Garces, it would have been only a matter of time before an investigation of the finance ministry revealed the millions of dollars diverted from the national treasury. Garces may have been a perverted bastard, but he had also been an ambitious man and a meticulous book-keeper. Somewhere within these stacks of records and computer tapes in the ministry was a list of international bank accounts and the names, as well as the amounts to which the missing funds had been diverted. At the very top of that list could be found the names of two of the province's leading military men. They now stood before him. And of course, his name, and that of practically everyone else at the governor's party were on that list as well. When Garces's body had been discovered he had panicked and phone Parros and Rivas. They had both arrived at the same time, and realizing the seriousness of the situation, had adjourned to the study. Here in this room was where the insane plan had been developed.

The raid on the house had obviously been carried out by a well-trained military unit of Communist guerrillas. The killing of Garces in itself would have sparked little concern by the Americans. But it had been the abduction of Paul Bracken that had provided the key to set the plan into motion.

Bracken's bodyguard, Highfield, had already notified the embassy and they, in turn, had notified the State Department. This had been followed immediately by an urgent request from Duran to President Pizarro that American assistance be requested. By exaggerating the seriousness of the situation and escalating the number of guerrillas roaming the mountains of his province, he was able to convince the President to make such a request. That decision had played into the hands of General Parros. He knew the American response would take at least a week. In the meantime, every terrorist act that occurred in the country could be placed on the doorstep of the Communists, including the total destruction of the finance ministry. It had seemed like the perfect plan at the time. The Americans would assist in the destruction of the Communist guerrillas that had been slowly but surely infiltrating into Ecuador and any records that Garces had hidden away would go up in smoke with the ministry. But then the unexpected had happened. Captain Sanchez had found and rescued Paul Bracken. To make matters worse, the American had not been harmed in any way. The United States would halt all troop preparation and things would return to normal once again.

It was at this point that General Parros had decided to risk it all, his logic being that he had little to lose. The new Ecuadorian president had already issued notice that any official, civilian or military, convicted of corruption, would be executed immediately after trial.

Duran forced down the tequila. It did little to settle his queasy stomach. The governor was terrified of General Parros. Any man who could slaughter thirty of his own men would hardly hesitate to kill a province governor.

"Damn it, Duran!" screamed Parros, as he stepped to the bar and slapped the bottle of tequila to the floor, "I grow tired of this game. Why did you need to see us?"

Duran's heart was in his throat as he tried to spit out the question. "The—the killings in—Guayaquil. Why—why was that necessary?"

Colonel Rivas burst out in a laugh. "You sorry excuse for a man. You mean you have called us here for—for this stupid question? Ah, mi General, the man's ignorance is beyond belief."

Parros reached across the bar and grabbed Duran by the front of his silk shirt. Jerking him forward against the teakwood frame, he could feel the governor shaking like a small dog in a freezing rain. This pleased him. Staring at the scared little man through coal black eyes, he leaned to within inches of Duran's face. Duran went pale at the foul odor of Parros's breath.

"Listen to me, you little worm. I will explain this only once. We have to make it appear that the guerrillas have mounted a terrorist campaign throughout the country. The death of Captain Sanchez and his men was necessary to establish a pattern for the terrorist acts that will follow. The two Americans killed today were but another link in the chain. Tonight my men will destroy one of the oilfields outside of town. At the same time, other attacks will be made in Quito and Guayaquil. The targets will all be American. Now do you understand? When we destroy the ministry, it will appear to be the work of the guerrillas."

Parros's grip on Duran increased. The man's collar was choking him. Duran fluttered his eyelids to acknowledge that he understood.

Parros grinned, showing two rows of perfect white teeth, gleaming beneath a thick, black mustache. Releasing his hold on Duran, he shoved the breathless man back into the liquor cabinet, then turned and headed for the door. Duran gripped the edge of the bar to steady himself. Colonel Rivas was smiling as he shook his head slowly from side to side.

"You are muy loco, amigo. I do not think I would bother the general again. One can never tell when the guerrillas may return."

Still smiling, Rivas turned and followed Parros. Pausing at the door, he looked back over his shoulder and laughingly said, "Next time the guerrillas could be wearing our uniforms. Who can say? You have a nice day—Your Excellency."

Duran did not begin to breathe regularly until the oak door slammed shut behind the two officers. Grabbing another bottle of tequila from under the bar, he poured himself a very large drink, downing half the glass in the first gulp. He was still shaking, the cold, shark-eyed stare from Parros still fresh in his mind. Finishing the drink, he poured another. Sitting down on a bar stool, he thought of Paul Bracken. He wished now that he had given the man, Highfield, a car to drive Bracken back to his hotel instead of offering him a room at the mansion after the party. Paul Bracken had been a royal pain in the ass at times, and Lord knows they had exchanged heated words on more than one occasion, but the American didn't deserve this. Duran had a bad feeling that no matter how this affair turned out, Paul Bracken was a dead man.

Powers had taken his two new arrivals to the embassy. Now, standing before a huge map in the briefing room next to his office, the colonel pointed out the various locations of the day's events.

Mattson's attention was drawn immediately to the area in which the army patrol had been ambushed. Concentrating on the location for a moment, he stepped back and folded his arms. His eyes still locked onto the grid square, he asked, "Jake, do you notice anything peculiar about that ambush site?"

Jake moved closer to the map and focused in on the coordinates blocked in red. Looking at it from different angles, he turned to Mattson.

"Damn, B.J., there's something about it—I'm not sure what. That little warning light in the back of my mind keeps flashing, but I can't seem to—"

Colonel Powers now moved in on the area in question. After a few moments, he, too, turned to Mattson. "Major, what are you seeing that we don't?"

"Well, sir, I see two very complicated questions. For one, see where the bodies were found. Take a hard look at the terrain around the place, especially the relief lines along that ridge to the north."

Powers and Mortimer eyeballed it for a moment before Jake said, "OK. I've got a gentle flowing slope running down a ridge and also a main road on the west. I still don't get two questions out of that."

Powers raised his hand and rubbed his chin. The ridge and the road fixed in his eyes. Then it hit him.

"Wait a minute. If I had a guerrilla force that was large enough to take on a fully-equipped, thirty-man unit, I sure as hell wouldn't be moving them down a slope that open and straight toward a major road. There are no valleys or lower relief areas for cover and concealment."

"I'll be damned," said Jake. "Those boys would have to be awfully dumb to be moving in broad daylight."

"They're not dumb, Jake. They proved that by the way they took down the Governor's house. The thing that bothers me is why that area? And why during the day? Guerrillas don't take on a thirty-man outfit which is armed to the teeth, unless they outnumber them two or three to one. Now if that were the case, how in hell did they figure they could move sixty or ninety guys down that slope on a sunny afternoon with the army making a sweep through that open field to the south?"

"No, Major Mattson, that area to the south is where Captain Sanchez and his men were ambushed," reminded Powers.

"Ambushed from where, Colonel?" asked B.J., pulling on his lower lip.

The question threw Powers off balance for a moment. "Why—from the hill of course."

"Therein lies the second question, sir. How does one spring an effective ambush on a unit from four hundred yards away, and kill all thirty men?"

Jake's mouth dropped open at about the same time as Colonel Powers's.

"It's fucking impossible," said Jake.

"My feelings exactly, my man," smiled Mattson.

Powers grabbed the body recovery report from a desk next to the map and double-checked the coordinates. Mattson was right. From the base of the slope to where the bodies had been found was four hundred yards. And the hill was the only possible place in the immediate area where an ambush party could have been set up without being seen.

"I'll be damned," said Powers. "Just what the fuck happened out there?"

Mattson shook his head. "I don't know, Colonel. But whatever it was, it sure surprised the hell out of Captain Sanchez."

Jake glanced at his watch, then at Mattson. "B.J., we're burning up time we don't have. We've got less than fifteen hours to figure this thing out and relay to the general what we're going to need in here."

"Yeah, I know, Jake. Colonel, I'm sure you're aware that we're pressed for time. I realize you had a full briefing lined up for us but, if you wouldn't mind, could we take those folders with us, and you can fill us in on the way to the airport? We really need to get to Lago Agrio before dark."

"Of course, Major. I understand." Gathering up the folders on the briefing table, Powers shoved them into a briefcase, then called the embassy garage. As they made their way downstairs, he said, "You know, J. J. Johnson and I go back a long way. When he told me what he was planning to do, I figured he'd finally flipped. But having met you both, I see why he's the general, and I'm stuck down here."

"Well, Colonel, this doesn't seem like such a bad place," replied Jake.

"Let me tell you something, Commander. This may not be the asshole of the world, but you can get a damn good view of it from here."

The security for the drive to the airfield was the same as the trip to the embassy. Sergeant Maloy was shotgun in the front again.

"What about the President of this little wonderland?" asked Mattson. "Is he on the up and up, or can he be bought?"

"No way. He's as straight as they come. He would not, knowingly, stand for any corruption from the members of his government. He has already mandated that such actions will be dealt with in a swift trial, then execution. Too bad we don't have a few more like him around."

"Then why a revolution?" asked Jake, arching an eyebrow.

"I didn't say they aren't having their share of problems, Commander. You've got to remember. The military ran this country on and off for the last hundred years. A lot of those old generals still have influence within the government. President Pizarro is no fool. He knows things are far from being right. It took three hundred years for things to get this way. You can't expect a man to change them overnight. But at least he is trying. God, you wouldn't believe the progress he's made unless you'd been around to see the mess he inherited a year ago."

"OK," said B.J. "So what about this Lago Agrio? Who's in charge up there?"

The colonel nodded. "The place wasn't anything ten years ago. Texaco came in on an oil exploration trip and hit. Changed the whole financial structure of this country. Became a boom town overnight. Still puts out a lot of crude and makes a bundle for the country. The main man is supposed to be the province governor. His name is Miguel

Duran. Irritating attitude and a personality that only a mother could love. The guy's got 'crooked' written all over his face. He and Bracken didn't get along at all."

"Then why was Bracken at his party?" B.J. asked.

"Protocol, Major. The ambassador was supposed to go, but couldn't make it. He asked Bracken to stand in for him. Paul jumped at the chance, just to piss Duran off. As a matter of fact, when I heard that Paul had been snatched, my first thought was that Duran had staged the whole thing just to get rid of him."

"What changed your mind?" asked Jake.

Powers smiled "The look on the fucker's face when they brought Garces's body downstairs. I've seen my share of scared guys before, but Duran was petrified. He and Garces were close friends. If he had planned it, he wouldn't have killed his best friend. Especially like that!"

Mattson pulled a cigarette from his pocket and lighted it before saying, "You've got to admit, that was a classic piece of work they did on the boy."

"Yeah," said Jake. "I can see the coroner's report now. Cause of death: massive rectal expansion."

The comment drew a morbid laugh from everyone, including the driver.

"Any idea why they would have killed the man that way?"

"That's the only damn thing we are sure of, Major. Seems our boy Garces had an impotence problem when it came to the ladies. It took him hours to get it up. Somewhere along the line he found that he could cut the time with a little sadistic foreplay, especially with young girls, preferably virgins. Apparently, he was in the middle of one of his little torture sessions when the bad guys came on the scene. They seemed to have taken a rather dim view of the fat man's activities, and gave him a taste of his own medicine."

While Powers continued talking, Jake removed a folder from his bag and scanned through it quickly. When the colonel had finished, he said, "Colonel, this is supposed to be a copy of the original report sent to us by the embassy. There is no mention of any female involvement."

"Of course not, Commander. That is because there were no female bodies or personnel found at the governor's estate."

"Well how—"

"Mike Highfield; CIA and Bracken's bodyguard. He saw the bodies of two young Indian girls, in their teens, being removed from the house while he was on the phone with the embassy. Like I said, Duran is about as low as snake shit. We believe he was the procurer for the fat man. Not just those two girls, but as many as thirty or forty have come up missing in the last year and a half, but nobody will ever find them. You can bank on that."

"I would assume that Mister Highfield is soon to be without a job?" said B.J. as he cracked the window and flipped the cigarette away.

"I'm afraid so. Damn shame, too. Hell of a nice young man. Six years in the Marines, ran a force recon unit. Had tours all over the Middle East and in Europe. The Agency recruited him four years ago. He just had his twenty-ninth birthday last month. He thought of Paul more like a father than an assignment. But I'll tell you both something right now. For an old fart of fifty-five, Paul Bracken was a hard men to keep up with. He loved to party—and I mean all night. I guess Mike was just burnt out that night. He dozed off and didn't even hear Paul leave the room. That might have saved his life. You don't make mistakes with the Company, though one fuck-up and you're history."

"Yeah! I know a little bit about that," said Mattson. He chose not to elaborate on the subject. "Colonel, you said Duran was 'supposed' to be the man in charge?"

Removing the folder from his briefcase, he passed it across to Mattson.

"This is a complete dossier on the man behind the man. The real power in the province. His name is General Arturo Parros. Quite a remarkable career, actually. Heavily involved in the last two military coups, but shrewd enough to have maintained his power and position while others were either shot, jailed, or left the country. Don't be fooled by the man's charm. He's as ruthless and cold-blooded as they come. He rules Lago Agrio and the entire province with an iron fist. The boy doesn't fuck around, he deals with any problem situations on the spot. No trials, courts, or boards; none of that legal crap. He is the judge, jury, and executioner all in one. Four months ago, one of his units stumbled onto a small group of guerrillas camped along the Aquarico River. There were ten of them. It wasn't much of a firefight. The guerrillas only had three rifles in the bunch. The army patrol had forty. They like to do things in a big way down here. Anyway, they killed seven of them and captured three. That was unfortunate for the three. General Parros had them hung from trees by their wrists and their legs cut off at the knees with a machete. While they were screaming and squirting blood all over the place, he posed in front of them for a few pictures, then left them hanging there to bleed to death."

Mattson removed the general's photo from the folder, studied it for a moment, then passed it over to Mortimer.

"Boy looks like a real Harvard charmer, Jake."

"Nope. With a personality like that, sounds more like a Texas A & M product," said Jake, as he looked at the picture. "You know, he kind of resembles that other asshole down in Panama, only with a pussy tickler on his lips."

Powers grinned at the two men across from him. Johnson had chosen the right men for this job. They knew the seriousness of the situation, but still maintained a sense of humor. You had to in this business.

As the cars pulled onto the airfield, the blades of a UH1H Huey helicopter were just beginning to turn. The cars came to a stop a short distance away. As they got out, Powers said, "I'll radio Captain Jackson that you are on your way. Where do you want him to meet you?"

Mattson raised his voice to be heard over the increasing volume of the chopper.

"Is there an LZ or a pad at the governor's residence?"

Powers nodded that there was.

"That's where we'll go first. We'll be back here by 2100 hours. Could you have someone here to pick us up?"

Powers again nodded in the affirmative.

The crew chief waved for the two passengers to board. Jake grabbed their bags and climbed aboard the bird. Powers and Mattson shook hands and B.J. ran to climb aboard. The chopper reached lift-off RPMs and began to rise. The nose dipped and the helicopter shot forward rapidly, then rose swiftly, and banked left for the mountains to the northeast.

Sergeants Maloy and Rivers were standing by their cars as Powers returned. Glancing back once more at the disappearing helicopter, he turned to the two NCOs and said, "Well, boys, it'll be getting dark soon. We better get out to the ambassador's house and batten down the hatches. This could be a long night."

Young Captain Mark Jackson was waved through the wrought iron gates of the governor's estate by the soldiers on guard. Parking the car near the front steps, he and the two security men assigned to him by General Parros got out and waited to be cleared by more soldiers at the entrance. Governor Duran was not taking any chances on the guerrillas coming back for him.

From just beyond the mountains to the west, Jackson spotted the warning lights of Mattson's helicopter approaching. He breathed a sigh of relief. He had been afraid he would arrive too soon and have to indulge in small talk with the governor. Not that he knew enough about Duran to judge him one way or the other, the problem was his Spanish. The hundred bucks he had paid another student at the language school to switch IDs and take the test for him had already come back to haunt him. Colonel Powers had sent him to Lago Agrio with the promise that an intell team from the embassy would follow within hours. The threat to the embassy and Americans in the capital had changed all that. Jackson was on his own. Rather than admit to his new commander of only a few days that his language capabilities were far from those required for such a mission, he had simply boarded the chopper and flown to Lago Agrio. After all, he had learned some Spanish at the school and it was possible that he could tap dance his way through. That idea had gone down the tubes within fifteen minutes after his arrival.

He had been met at the helicopter pad by Colonel Rivas, all smiles and hand shakes, who then rattled off a sentence in Spanish so fast that Jackson hadn't understood one word of what the man said. Still trying to fake it, he meant to reply that it would be a pleasure to work with the colonel. Unfortunately it didn't come out that easy. Instead, what he told Rivas in smooth, distinct Spanish was that, "One should never pet a burning dog!" Captain Jackson's credibility had gone downhill from there. To show his contempt for the young American officer, Rivas made sure that the briefing scheduled for him had been given totally in Spanish, even though the officers conducting the briefing all spoke perfect English.

Having been in Lago Agrio for over fifteen hours, Captain Jackson knew no more now than he had when he arrived, a point that was not going to go over well with the two men about to land at the chopper pad next to the mansion.

Governor Duran stood on the lower balcony, flanked by two security men, and watched the chopper as it landed. Two tall Americans in civilian clothes stepped out and walked toward him. Another American, dressed in combat fatigues, suddenly appeared from around the corner of the balcony and met the two men halfway. Parros had told Duran about the young captain who had arrived from Quito to investigate the kidnapping, but he had not met him before this. Duran watched as the three Americans conferred for a few moments, then made their way to the balcony entrance. Smiling his best diplomatic smile, Duran greeted the three.

"Ah, gentlemen, words cannot express how glad I am to see you. General Parros and Colonel Rivas are on their way and should arrive momentarily. I am Miguel Duran, provincial governor of Lago Agrio."

Mattson extended his hand and made the introductions all around.

"If you will follow me, Major, we can wait in the study. I have an exceptionally well stocked bar, if any of you would care for a drink."

"That would be fine, sir," replied Mattson. Jake and B.J. both noticed Duran slightly glazed eyes and could clearly smell the strong odor of tequila. The governor was already half in the bag. Once in the study, everyone was seated and drinks prepared.

"Nasty business, this kidnapping of our friend, Paul Bracken. He and I were quite close, you know. I am certainly glad to see your government is wasting no time in coming to our assistance. When do you suppose your troops will be arriving, Major Mattson?" asked Duran as he took a long drink from his tequila-filled glass. Jake slowly swirled the ice around in his glass, then glanced over at B.J. Close friends, indeed.

"Well, sir, that's hard to say. I'm afraid I can't give you an answer on that. You see, we are more like an advance planning team. We first have to evaluate requirements for deployment. Of course, our primary concern is for the safe return of Mr. Bracken."

"Of course. I can fully appreciate that. However, I am sure you are aware of the events of the past few hours. General Parros feels that the Communist's are preparing for a full-scale takeover throughout the country. Surely, your president will not allow such a thing. He must send troops to help us. Our army is small and although many have been trained by your Special Forces Mobile Training Team, we are no match for these Cuban led guerrillas."

"Are you certain they are led by Cubans?"

"Yes. One of Colonel Rivas's commando teams captured one of them a few weeks ago. He was definitely a Cuban."

"When could we talk with this Cuban, Governor? He could provide very important information for us."

"I'm afraid that will not be possible, Major Mattson. Colonel Rivas has already conducted an interrogation of the man. He refused to answer any of the colonel's questions. To the very end, I might add. The poor fellow hung himself in his cell only a few nights ago."

There was just a hint of sarcasm in Mortimer's tone as he

quietly said, "Yes, I imagine that sort of thing happens quite often."

Duran stared suspiciously at Jake and started to ask what he was implying, when the doors swung open and General Parros and Colonel Rivas entered the room. Walking straight to the three Americans, Parros reached out his hand. "Gentlemen, I am sorry for the delay, but with this situation as it is, I have to make sure that my forces are prepared for any possible action by the guerrillas tonight. I am sure you understand."

Mattson shook hands with both officers and noticed the concerned look in Parros's eyes when he saw Duran was drinking. "Now, Major, how can I assist you?" asked the general.

"We are going to need to know the estimated strength of the guerrilla force you are up against, as well as their suspected areas of concentration. I would also like any information you may have obtained in the past few hours in reference to Mr. Bracken," replied B.J.

General Parros placed his hands on his hips and began to strut about the room. Rivas stood silently next to the bar, near Duran.

"Major, we are certain we are dealing with a very large and well armed Communist force led by Cuban advisers. I would put their strength at possibly, eight to nine thousand."

The numbers given stunned even Duran, who nearly dropped his drink.

Jake and Mattson exchanged glances before Mortimer said, "Sir, we were provided with intelligence reports that related to the guerrilla activities in this area over the last two or three years. According to those reports, there has only been an occasional incident of a few telephone poles or a bridge blown up here and there. I find it hard to believe that a force of that size would restrict their activities to such minor acts."

"Ah! But you see, Commander, they have been planning for some time to launch their major assault. The killing of Minister Garces and the kidnaping of Mr. Bracken were the first actions signaling the start of larger, more devastating attacks that are to begin throughout the country. My army is a brave one, but I fear they are no match for the ruthless, no-quarter type of fighting that will be required to rid my province and the country of these Communists. That is why U.S. assistance is required immediately."

Carefully, B.J. replied, "General, what you are asking is going to be very difficult. As you know, the five Central American countries met in Costa Rica a few days ago and signed a declaration of peace. President Ortega of Nicaragua held a press conference and made a point of stating that now that there is peace in Central America, and I quote, 'The Yankee Imperialists will now find it necessary to search out another Latin country in which to practice their greed for world expansion and exploitation,' end quote. So you see, general, any action by the President must be weighed heavily against the criticism that is sure to arise from a massive U.S. troop buildup in your country."

"Fuck criticism, Major. U.S. support is needed in my country, and it is needed now. I am aware that our President Pizarro has already requested such assistance. My question to you is, why hasn't your government acted on that request?"

"I am sure it is being considered at the highest level, even as we talk."

Parros's voice began to rise in irritation. "Talk? What good is talk? Our governor's home is attacked, your Mr. Bracken is kidnapped, a minister and a number of others are killed, and they find it necessary to just talk! Thirty of my finest soldiers were killed this morning." Parros paused and made the sign of the cross before he continued, his voice filled with false emotion. "Captain Sanchez was a fine young officer and like a son to me. He and all of his men were butchered trying to find your Mr. Bracken; but still they càn only talk."

Rivas watched in wonder at the show his general was putting on for the Americans. Captain Jackson seemed to be buying the act. If the other two did, they weren't showing it.

"Just what does it take to make your president realize the seriousness of this situation? Perhaps if it had been thirty American soldiers that had been machine gunned—" Parros suddenly stopped himself. A look of panic leaped across Riva's face. Duran's glass slipped from his hand and shattered on the marble floor.

Ignoring the breaking glass and fixing his eyes on Parros, B.J. said, "Go on, General. You were about to say machine gunned, I believe. Is that how Captain Sanchez and his unit were wiped out? A machine gun ambush?"

Small beads of sweat had appeared along Parros's forehead. He had gotten so carried away in his oratory that he had made a mistake. and he knew it. A mistake that had now raised unwanted questions from the American major.

"Why, yes, Major. Some—some of the men had been killed by machine gun fire. These guerrillas are well armed, as I said earlier."

"We found hundreds of shells casings littering the ground at the ambush site. They had perhaps three or four machine gun positions," added Rivas.

"We haven't had an opportunity to see the area of the ambush, Colonel," said Jake, "but a guerrilla unit that would carry even three machine guns would have to be fairly large in size. Was there enough cover for them to hide a unit that big?"

Now Colonel Rivas began to sweat. He had been sent to kill the men, not do a study of the land. The open field in which they had gunned down the unit was all he could remember. The surrounding terrain had not been important. His hesitation in answering Mortimer's question was serving only to increase the Americans' suspicions. He had to say something. "There are a vast number of ravines and hills around the entire area, Commander. Why the young captain chose to lead his men into such rugged terrain without securing the high ground is beyond me."

The answer had obviously pleased both Parros and Rivas. Duran, on the other hand, had suddenly appeared as nervous as a cat on a hot tin roof. Something wasn't right here, and Mattson and Jake knew it.

General Parros, feeling that Rivas's answer had corrected his near blunder, said, "Now, gentlemen, if you will come with me, we shall go to my headquarters and I can show you those areas that we feel are presently being used by the guerrilla forces. Colonel Rivas, will you escort the officers to the car? I would like a word with the governor."

"Certainly, sir. Gentlemen, if you will follow me—"

All three men stood as B.J. told Jake and Jackson to go ahead. Stepping in front of Duran, he shook the man's hand. Duran's palms were sweating and there was a worried look in his eyes as Mattson said, "Thank you for your time, Governor. I am sure we will be seeing each other again."

Duran tried to smile and nodded his head. "Of course, Major."

As soon as Mattson had left the room, Parros turned to Duran and slapped the man off the bar stool. "You drunken bastard! You have guilt written all over your face. I do not want to see you drinking any more until this thing is over. Do you understand me?"

Duran looked up from the floor. His hand against his burning left cheek. He nodded that he understood as Parros turned on his heel and stomped from the room. Duran was a weak man and Parros had no use for weak men. The governor was a liability that he could no longer afford. By the time the doors to the study had closed, Parros had made his decision. Duran would have to be killed.

Arriving at Parros's headquarters, Mattson noticed the marked difference between the appearance of the soldiers under Parros's command and the Ecuadorian troops they had seen at the airport and around the embassy. Their uniforms had been worn and slightly faded. That was not the case with Parros's troops. In fact, they appeared to be new uniforms, neatly pressed and with a brightly colored insignia of a skull with crossed lances behind it. The patch had been designed by Parros himself and was worn only by the soldiers of his command. The jungle boots they wore were new and highly polished. Whereas the regular soldiers of this country's military carried only M-16 rifles, Parros's men carried a variety of weapons. All had side arms attached to new pistol belts and holsters. There were .45s, 9mm Berettas, and even a few Walther PPKs.

The automatic weapons ran from MP-5s to Car-15 assault rifles. Nearly all these weapons were far from the standard issue of the Ecuadorian military forces. Where had Parros gotten them? Better yet, how had he paid for them? Not only did Parros's army look better dressed and better equipped, but they apparently were better paid. Of the ten to twelve soldiers they passed in the hall on the way to the briefing room, each wore either a gold necklace, gold ring, or gold bracelet. Some wore all three. In a country where the average soldier made about forty dollars a month, these boys were well paid by someone. And that someone was General Parros. What he had, in effect, was his own private army, and a damn well equipped one, at that.

For the next hour and a half, Parros and Rivas produced report after report of guerrilla activities that had occurred throughout the country over the past three years, placing particular importance on the need for U.S. assistance at every opportunity. By the time they finished, they had made it sound as thought nothing short of another Grenada invasion was needed in Ecuador. Mattson and Mortimer were far from convinced. Each time the subject of Bracken was brought up, Parros or Rivas gave assurances that the man was certain to be found in due time. B.J. finally had enough of the seemingly never ending reports and informed the general that they were going to have to return to the capitol. They would pass the information they had received on to Washington, but could not guarantee what action would be taken.

In the meantime, Mattson would like to bring in a couple of Special Forces teams and join the search for the consul general. Would the general have any objections? At first the request had brought a look of disgust from Parros. He wanted massive intervention, not just a couple of A-Teams. Then, just as quickly, his attitude seemed to change. Of course he and his men would welcome the assistance of such highly trained professionals. When could they expect them? Mattson stated they could be here within twenty-four hours. "By all means then, Major, we await their arrival," said Parros, as a confused Colonel Rivas looked on.

The helicopter had relocated to the airfield at the far end of Parros's headquarters compound. Parros and Rivas walked with the three men as far as their cars and then bade them farewell, until tomorrow afternoon, when they could expect the Special Forces teams to arrive. Until then, the general's troops would continue the search on their own. Mattson thanked them and their cars headed for the chopper pad. During the short ride, Jackson started to say, "You know, I'm sort of new at this, but there's something awfully funny about the way the gener—"

Jake cut the young captain off. "Captain, could you please be quiet? I'm trying to think." Jackson was shocked by the abrupt interruption, until he saw Jake move his head from side to side then nod toward the soldier that was driving the car. Everything that was said by the three would be repeated to Parros as soon as they left. Jackson signaled silently that he understood and sat back in the seat.

Within five minutes they were airborne and on their way back to Quito. They would arrive a little before 2100 hours. Colonel Powers, being the efficient officer he appeared to be, would have their transportation at the airfield, no matter what time they arrived.

Jackson had confided to Mattson and Mortimer his short comings in dealing with Rivas, and his lack of enough language ability to accomplish anything of value in Lago Agrio. B.J. had thought it better that the young captain return to the capitol with them. There was something very strange going on in that province. Too many things didn't make sense. It was no place for an American who could not understand what was being said.

The side doors of the helicopter were closed against the cold night air. Staring out at the glittering lights of Quito in the distance, B. J. Mattson was sunk deep in thought. He was going to have to call General Johnson from the embassy. They would use the secure phone system to MacDill. But what was he going to tell him?

Bracken was still missing. The governor was a crook and front man for a powerful general with his own private army.

That same general had lied about guerrilla strength in his area, lied about circumstances surrounding the death of thirty of his own soldiers, and seemed too confident that Paul Bracken was alive and well. So confident in fact, that one would suspect he had firsthand knowledge of where the man was. OK, so what do you make out of all that? The question kept going around in his head. No matter how many times he tried to put it all together, it came out the same. It just didn't make any sense. Why was Parros so insistent on a U.S. buildup? Why had Rivas lied about the terrain around the ambush site? Why had Duran dropped his glass and turned pale when Parros mentioned machine guns and the late Captain Sanchez in the same breath?

Questions and more questions. But General Johnson was not going to want questions; he needed answers. That was why they were here. For the moment, Mattson had no answers, only a long list of disturbing questions. Sitting across from him, he could see the faraway look in Jake's eyes. The commander was doing the same thing, searching for answers to a confusing puzzle that refused to come together. Lighting a cigarette, Mattson let the smoke curl slowly from his lips. Instinct told him that Duran knew more than he was telling. Tomorrow, when they returned with the Special Forces teams, he intended to get the man alone. Without Parros standing over him, Duran could be made to talk more freely. That would provide him with some of the answers, but not all. The remaining answers to the puzzle would have to be found in the dense jungles below. They would have to search out and find the guerrillas. Smashing out the cigarette on the floor, Mattson removed a pad and pen from his shirt pocket and began drafting a plan of operation.

• • •

General Parros made one last inspection of the men Rivas had hand picked to destroy one of the oil tank farms and the pipeline. They were dressed in a mix and match of faded jeans and uniforms. Russian AK-47s hung loosely from their shoulders. Satisfied that all was in order, he bade them good luck and sent them off into the darkness. Colonel Rivas watched them as the last man disappeared beyond the wire. Turning to Parros, he asked, "General, why did you consent to the major's request to bring in the Special Forces teams? They could interfere with the other operations we have planned."

Parros smiled. "Colonel, you heard what he said about the pressure that had been placed on their president due to the Central American treaty. He was right. The American people would not stand for intervention here. They enjoy thinking of themselves as the peacemakers. The Contras are gone and now they believe they have achieved lasting peace in Central America. They are an egotistical country of hypocritical fools. On the one hand they preach peace, but let an incident such as the Marine barracks bombing in Beirut, or the hanging of a hostage occur, and they are ready to start World War Three. Apparently they do not take our situation here seriously. Therefore, since their president fears action because of the American people's opinions, I shall provide him with the necessary motivation to change that opinion. Or, I should say, Major Mattson and his Green Berets will."

A bewildered look came over Colonel Rivas's face as he said, "How will this be, mi General?"

"Quite simple, my friend. Tomorrow afternoon Major Mattson and his Special Forces shall meet the same fate as did Captain Sanchez. Let us see how the Americans react when it is their soldiers who have been slaughtered like sheep. We shall provide plenty of pictures, of course. The bloodier the better. The American press enjoys blood and gore."

"You are indeed a brilliant man, General."

"I know," said Parros, as he looked toward the oilfields to the south of Lago Agrio. Rubbing his hands together to warm them from the cold, he remarked, "It is a lovely night for a fire."

CHAPTER 7

General Johnson switched the push to talk mike phone to secure.

"Secure mode locked. Go ahead, Major."

"Sir, we have just returned from Lago Agrio. Had an interesting visit with the province governor and the area commander. We haven't been able to get a positive lead on Mr. Bracken, but we feel strongly that he is still alive. Sir, I realize you have to contact the President in less than ten hours. I wish we could give you more to go on, but I'm sure you're aware that things have heated up a bit down here."

Johnson knew the odds had been a hundred to one that his two officers would be able to walk right in and pick up Bracken's trail, but he had hoped that, just by chance, they could beat those odds. They hadn't. "B.J., how do you and the commander evaluate the situation?"

Mattson paused a moment and looked over at Jake. "Do we tell him how we figure it, or do we just go by the facts?" he asked.

"Hell, B.J., we haven't seen any reliable facts since we've been here. Our evaluation can't be any worse than then anyone else's. Go with it."

"General Johnson, sir, Jake and I have studied this damn

thing from every possible angle and reached the conclusion that there's something about this situation that smells. Nothing about it fits the scenario."

"Like what, Major? And be specific."

Mattson ran down the list he had made in the chopper. The misinformation, the exaggeration of numbers, the overall nervousness of nearly everyone they had spoken with, and finally the suspicious nature and circumstances by which Captain Sanchez and his men had met their demise. The sudden violent attacks by guerrillas who before had been content with making nasty speeches and blowing an occasional telephone pole. No, something wasn't right down here and the governor and General Parros were ankle deep in the shit.

Johnson had waited until B.J. finished before saying, "Are you trying to tell me that it was not the guerrillas that were responsible for Bracken's kidnapping, Major?"

"No sir, not at all. I believe the takedown of the house was engineered by them, but I am beginning to have my doubts about exactly who they were after. I don't think it was Bracken. Possibly the minister, or the governor, but I'm not positive on that yet. Jake and I both feel that Governor Duran is hiding something. The man is scared to death of this General Parros. And from what we've heard, he has plenty of reason to be."

"What about the Bendix killings today?"

"Possibly a guerrilla hit, but we don't think so."

"Explain, Major."

"General, as you know the key to any successful guerrilla action is surprise. Guerrillas don't phone embassies and announce they are going to blow them up. Somebody down here did exactly that."

Johnson asked Mattson to hold for a minute. He had another call. Jake asked, "What'd he say?"

"He hasn't really said anything yet. Just listening."

The general was back on the line. "B.J. That was the secretary of defense on the other line. Seems I underestimated our boy. Sweet tracked you both down faster than I thought he could. The secretary wanted to know who authorized your solo trip to Ecuador without approval by Sweet or the JCS. I told him I did. He was pissed and reminded me that Sweet is to be kept up to date on your every move down there. The bastards on the hill are starting to apply pressure. They want an immediate airlift of troops to Ecuador for the protection of all American civilians. It's all politically motivated, I'm afraid. The Democrats saw Ortega's speech after the treaty signing. They want to push the President into committing U.S. troops, then they'll stand back and cut him to pieces for doing it. So much for 'a more gentle and caring nation.' "

"Sounds like the same crap they did to President Johnson over Vietnam. Is he going to go along with them, sir?" asked Mattson.

"He sure as hell doesn't want to. But every time some asshole down there shoots at an American, you better believe the outcry goes up two more notches on the Richter scale. Sweet has been getting calls all night from the Pentagon. The other branches are foaming at the mouth to get in down there. Tell me, Major, do we have any chance of finding Bracken before this shit hits the fan?"

"Sir, if you will authorize the immediate deployment of two Special Forces A-Teams, I believe we can give it a damn good run. I would recommend that the two teams come from the 3rd of the 7th Special Forces out of Panama, rather than Fort Bragg. They're closer, and it would save considerable time."

"I agree," said Johnson. "I'll get a flash message off to

them as soon as we hang up. Are there two teams you want in particular?"

"Well, sir, Kenny McMillan is the battalion sergeant major down there. He'd know who had the hottest teams running. I'd like for him to pick them and come along for the fun, if he can."

"OK B.J., you'll have him and the teams in the country by noon tomorrow. Is there anything or anyone else you need?"

Mattson thought about it for a moment, then asked, "Yes sir, as a matter of fact, there is. Could we possibly get Master Sergeant Smith and two of our own chopper crews from the aviation section? We're going to have to put in a lot of blade time and I'd feel a hell of a lot better with our own people behind those machine guns on the birds. Nancy will kill me when I get back, but Tommy will love it."

"No problem, Major. Anything else?"

"No, sir. That about covers it. If you can convince the President to hold back the wolves for at least the next seventy-two hours, I believe we can unscramble this jigsaw puzzle and recover Mr. Bracken, sir."

"I'm glad to see you haven't lost your optimism, major. I certainly hope it's valid. Otherwise, this time next week I'll be raising pigs on a farm in Alabama. We'll do what we can here. Have Colonel Powers keep us informed, and good luck, Major."

Mattson flipped the secure switch off and put down the phone.

"Well?" asked Jake.

"We had better get some sleep, Commander. Tomorrow we start work, jungle style."

Mortimer let out a yell. "All right! Brother, it can't be soon enough for me. God, I love this business."

Leaving the radio section, they made their way upstairs to

a small room that Powers had ordered prepared for the overnight stay of their two visitors. A bottle of Jack Daniel's, the seal unbroken, sat on a small, makeshift table. There could no longer be any doubt. Colonel Robert Powers was definitely one hell of an efficient officer.

General Sweet left the mission preparation room and went into his office. Turning on the small night-light on his desk, he picked up the phone and punched up the special number, waiting patiently as it rang for a third time. A familiar voice answered midway through the fourth ring.

"Hello."

"Contact has been made."

The voice seemed more attentive now. "Have they found him?"

"No. Not yet. They have requested two Green Beret teams from Panama for assistance."

"Can we stop that or at least stall them until we are ready to make our move?"

"I doubt it. Bracken is a personal friend of the President's, remember. He will be willing to try anything, short of mass deployment, if he thinks there is a chance. If we try to hold up those teams, Johnson will go straight to the man. We could get caught in the middle."

There was a pause at the other end of the line; then, "Suggestions."

"Let the teams go in. It's a big ass country. What difference could it possibly make? Major Mattson is hunting for a needle in a haystack. It'll take more than a couple dozen hotshot Green Beanies to find it."

"Agreed. We expect to receive additional support for the deployment demand by morning. A few of our friends in congress are hosting a private party tonight. They have invited only those colleagues they feel can be swayed to our side. The momentum is building, General. Are you prepared to activate the immediate response units once we go to full alert?"

"Absolutely, sir. I have all required codes and lock-in phrases prepared. I have already brought the commander of the 82nd Airborne Division to a code yellow, standby. Pope Air Force Base is holding in the same status and the necessary aircraft are in position for lift-off of the paratroopers."

"Is General Johnson aware of these preparations?"

"Not yet, sir. My sources in the communications section at Fort Bragg are deliberately delaying all inquires made by the Special Warfare Center in reference to the activities going on at Pope. Likewise, my people in command signal here are holding all incoming traffic from Bragg and the Ranger Units in Georgia until I have personally cleared it. All I need is the go signal from your end, sir. By the time General Johnson realizes what has happened, we will have the 82nd Airborne in the air and halfway to Ecuador."

"Excellent work, General. All we need now is for the Communists to blow up a few U.S. corporate buildings and kill a few more Americans, and we'll be in there. Even the President can't ignore a mandate by the entire congress and senate. We'll prove once and for all that there is no need for this overrated Special Operations Command. Keep me informed and be prepared to launch on our directive. Good-bye, General."

General Parros's commandos moved out of the jungle darkness and to a position near the heavy chain link fence on the east side of the Texaco tank farm. The huge, round, metal storage tanks of Oilfield Number Three were full to the brim with Ecuador's black gold.

Wire cutters were used to snip an opening in the wire.

The small team worked its way along the inner fence until they came to the first tank. Silently, and with a precision born of experience, they placed the first charge.

It was four A.M. when the Marine guard banged on the door. There was trouble in Lago Agrio. Colonel Powers wanted them in the operations room immediately. Still only half awake, B.J. and Jake dressed and made their way downstairs to the operations room. Powers was yelling into the mike of one of the radios when they entered the room.

"Goddamn it, Hendricks, we're supposed to be working together on this thing! Now we both know you've got agents working in Agrio. I know they've already reported what's going on out there, so let's knock off this secret agent shit and you tell me what happened, okay?"

Powers saw Mattson and Mortimer enter the room. While waiting for Hendricks to reply, he nodded and pointed to a back room and a large coffee pot. That was exactly what they needed.

Powers was taking notes as he slowly but surely drew the needed information from Rick Hendricks, the CIA station chief in Ecuador. The operations complex had become a beehive of activity. Teletypes were pounding out a flood of traffic, and a bank of radios against one wall, which had been set to Ecuadorian military frequencies, screeched and came to life with excited voices bursting forth in rapid Spanish. B.J. managed to catch part of one of the conversations over the clatter and noise of the room. There had been a series of explosions and something about fires out of control. Taking a sip from his cup of steaming coffee, Jake quickly pulled the cup away from his mouth.

"Damn, this shit is hot!" Blowing on the coffee, he glanced over at his partner as he said, "They hit the oilfields didn't they?"

"Looks that way. I just hope that's all they hit. This is

going to make it tough on the ol' man and the President to restrain the brass."

"I hear that," replied Jake, as he brought the cup back up to his lips, then thought better of it.

Colonel Powers had stopped writing. "Thanks Rick, sorry I got a little tense with you. Guess I need to get laid. Talk to you later."

Jake and B.J. joined the colonel by the radio. "What have we got, sir?"

"Somebody cut their way into the oil farm. Blew three of the tanks. The fire is out of control and spreading fast. They've got a total of seven storage tanks in that sector and it looks like they're going to lose them all."

"Casualties?" asked Mattson.

"Five government troopers killed, four wounded."

"Any Americans?"

Powers threw his pad and pencil on a desk. "Yeah, afraid so. Three that were working in that sector confirmed killed and possibly two more. They're not sure. They were just leaving the sector when the first tank went up. It's too hot for them to get in there and confirm. But they don't think they made it."

"Well, that rips it," said Jake. "It's exactly what the assholes on the hill wanted. Within the next forty-eight hours they'll be coming in here with everything they've got."

Powers sat down on the corner of his desk and rubbed his head. "God, I hate this shit. If they come roaring in here, we're going to play right into Communist hands. Hell, Daniel Ortega will call a major press conference in Nicaragua just so he can point a finger at us and say, 'See, We told you so.' Damn it, don't those shitbirds on the hill realize what they'll be doing? We don't have a full-scale revolution yet, but if they come in here shooting the shit out of everything and everybody, we'll have one hell of a revolution on our hands by the end of the week. Not to mention the fact that they'll string up Paul Bracken to the nearest tree."

Mattson looked at his watch, then asked, "Colonel, do you have the frequencies for U.S. Southern Command, and the 7th Special Forces Group in Panama?"

"Of course."

"Okay, sir. I would suggest that we get on the radio and get this show on the road. We need to inform 7th Group to skip the normal load out list and get over to Howard Air Base. I'm sure they've already laid on transport, but you may have to push South Com to move everything up to priority immediate. They give you any shit, tell 'em it's authorized by the Commander of SOCOM and the President of the United States. I don't think the joint chiefs would be foolish enough to interfere, but they may try and stall the movement. It won't hurt to put a little ball twisting on them. Jake and I are going by to pick up your boy, Jackson. We'll need everybody we can get."

"Colonel, you have an Ecuadorian Special Forces Brigade here, don't you?" asked Jake.

"Why, yes we do."

"How good are they?"

"Hell, they're the only real army in this country. Every one of them hand picked and trained by Special Forces Mobile Training Teams from Fort Bragg."

"Who's the commander?" asked B.J.

"Colonel Ramon Escobar: Airborne, SF, and Ranger qualified."

"Can he be trusted?"

"If you mean does he have any connections with the generals, past and present, I'd have to say no. He's pretty much his own man." Powers paused a moment, then said,

"You don't think it is guerrillas doing this, do you Major?"

"Let's just say I have some serious doubts. Can you get in contact with Colonel Escobar and inform him that Jake and I would like to meet with him at his headquarters as soon as possible?"

"You've got it. Anything else?"

"Sorry if I seem to be taking over, Colonel. Bad habit, I guess."

"Not at all, Major. You and the commander here seem to be the only two that have any idea of what the fuck is going on. As the old saying goes, I got the track and if you want to drive the train, then knock yourself out."

"Thank you, sir. If you can take care of all of that, we'll get Jackson and head for Escobar's headquarters. Could we get a couple of the hand-held radios set on the embassy frequencies to carry with us? That way we can maintain contact with you. I'll need to know when the teams are arriving."

"No problem, B.J." Yelling to one of his radio operators to secure two radios for the men, Powers went to work on contacting Southern Command in Panama. Jake and B.J. ran upstairs and gathered up the few belongings they had brought with them, including the bottle of Jack.

By the time they returned downstairs, a driver and a jeep were waiting outside the embassy. Jake made a communications check with the hand-held radios to assure they had contact, then instructed the driver to head for Captain Jackson's quarters. From here on out time was going to be a factor.

High in their mountain stronghold above the Napo River, Colonel Suplao and Joaquin Ochoa stood silently in the darkness and stared at the bright red-orange glow that lighted the sky to the east of Lago Agrio. Carlos Cruz joined the two men and said, "That must be a very large fire to light up the sky so brightly, mi Coronel."

"Yes, Carlos, it is in the vicinity of the tank farm. It can only be an oil fire. Did either of you hear the distant sound of the explosions?"

"Si mi Coronel, there were three," answered Ochoa.

"I fail to understand what is happening here, Joaquin. The news broadcast earlier had no mention of the recovery of the consul general. Only news of the slaughter of government soldiers and the killing of the Americans. Now someone has blown up the oilfields. But who? We gave no such orders. All of our men are accounted for, and besides, none of our groups would dare such operations without informing me. Who is doing these things?"

Ochoa continued to study the blazing sky and said, "I have no idea, sir. But no matter, we are sure to be the ones that will be blamed for these actions. Of that you may be assured."

"Yes. I realize that. Fidel will—" As if by some strange magic, the mention of the Cuban leader's name brought the camp radio man.

"Sir, Fidel is on the radio. He wishes to talk with you immediately."

Suplao felt his stomach tighten. He already knew the questions he would be asked. He had no answers. Their plan for revolution was far from being a secret any longer. Ochoa and Cruz watched as their commander walked into the radio hut. "What do you think Fidel will want us to do now, Joaquin?"

"I am not sure, Carlos. The whole world will know we are here in a few hours. We have fewer than seven hundred men organized. I would hope that Suplao could convince Fidel to let us withdraw. Otherwise, I fear we shall have to face the American airborne soldiers that are sure to arrive soon."

"Not a pleasant thought, Joaquin. I was on Grenada when they came. Their firepower is unbelievable. They have a huge gunship they call a spectre. It fires 20mm Gatling guns and even a 40mm cannon. When it flew over us it was as if hell had come to visit. No, I have no desire to face such an aircraft again."

Ochoa saw Suplao come out of the radio shack. "Perhaps you will not have to, my old friend. Suplao has finished his conversation with Fidel."

Both men waited patiently as the commander stopped and issued orders to three of his officers. He then walked up to them.

"Fidel is very upset about the unfortunate turn of events here. If he had his way, we would be left on our own to face the Americans as well as the Ecuadorian forces. But that is not the view of our Russian allies. Fidel did not say as much, but I believe they have pressured our leader into recalling our forces back to Nicaragua. The planned infiltration of five hundred men that had been scheduled for tonight has been aborted. We are to cache all excess weapons and ammunition and move our forces across the Putumayo River into Colombia, where we will link up with our brothers of the Colombian Liberation Front. They will provide us with transportation to the coast, there to be picked up by freighter late tomorrow night. Major Ochoa, you will secure all data on our Ecuadorian comrades. We will need that information when we return to this country. That may be in six months, it may be in six years, but you can be certain we will be back. Now, go on. I must try to explain to our friends why we have to leave so suddenly, although I am sure they will not understand."

Ochoa saluted and moved out for the operations tent. He

found himself whistling a gay tune as he began gathering the files. In less than seventy-two hours he would be back in his beloved Cuba, and in the arms of his beautiful, raven-haired wife whom he had not seen for over a year. Ironically, this had been made possible by a mistake on his part: the kidnapping of Paul Bracken.

Securing the last of the papers, he stuck them into a leather briefcase and walked outside. The predawn gray of morning had broken on the horizon. To the east the fire had turned the sky a blood red. Ochoa paused and thought of the consul general. Where was the American who had ultimately become their benefactor? Why had he not been found?

General Parros smiled to himself as he watched the changing colors of red and orange dance in the sky beyond the town. Everything was going as planned. He could only imagine the turmoil his actions would cause in Washington. Perhaps the oil fire would be enough. No, the Americans would need something more solid on which to vent their rage. The killing of the Special Forces teams would assure a rapid reaction. He was still admiring the work of his commandos when Colonel Rivas joined him.

"General, your security officer has radioed that Mr. Bracken is awake and has been attempting to remove his blindfold. He demands that he be released at once. They wish instruction, sir."

"Aah, yes. Mr. Bracken. I had considered killing him along with the other Americans, but now that I have had time to ponder the matter I believe I have a better idea. It is said that the American president is a close friend of our Mr. Bracken. No doubt he is deeply concerned. What better way for me to gain favor with the president and the American people, than by being the one that rescues the poor man from his terrible ordeal."

Rivas seemed puzzled by his commander's words. "Just how will you accomplish that, General?"

"That is your only failing grace, my dear Rivas. You have no imagination. We simply hold on to him until the Americans have been in our country for a few days; we let them mount a massive search, then we stage a firefight for the benefit of the blindfolded diplomat. He will hear the firing, we rush in and save him. Not only is he grateful, but I am a hero as well."

"You are a wise man, mi General. But what if the Americans that were here yesterday should accidentally discover where Mr. Bracken is being held? You would be hard pressed to explain why he was on your property."

"Yes, you are right of course. That American major, what was his name?"

"Mattson, sir."

"Yes. Major Mattson. I noticed a certain skepticism in his eyes yesterday during the briefings. Perhaps we had better move our guest to a more secluded hideaway. How many men do we have at my ranchero?"

"Perhaps thirty-five or forty men, sir," replied Rivas.

"Good. That should be sufficient. Inform the officer in charge that he is to take all the men and the American to Esmeraldas. I will arrange for the necessary seaplanes to transport them to Genovesa."

Rivas seemed surprised at the name. "Genovesa, sir!"

"Yes, Colonel, and tell that officer that if the American is seen by even one person before they get there, I will personally blow his brains out. Now go."

Rivas clicked his heels, saluted smartly, and turned to leave.

"One other thing, Colonel. Tell him that once on Genovesa, he is to have his men dress as guerrillas. If Mr. Bracken should get his blindfold off, it would not do for him to see his captors in our uniforms. When you have accomplished that, report back here. I have one more job for your commandos."

"Yes, sir. I will tell him." Saluting again, Rivas left for the communications room.

Turning back to observe the brilliant colors that had been reflected in the sky, Parros was disappointed to find that they were gone, replaced now by a clear blue sky and a rising sun. A large cloud of black smoke curled its way upward from the burning oilfield. Placing his hands behind his back he rocked comfortably on his heels, his mind envisioning the day's planned events. Major Mattson would arrive with his Green Berets. They would be given a false report of an enemy sighting and location. When they went to investigate, they would be ambushed and killed by a company of Colonel Rivas's Rangers. It would only be fitting that they die at the hands of fellow paratroopers. He had already prepared his message of condolence that would be delivered to the U.S. embassy after the deed had been done.

At the end of the heartfelt letter he had mentioned the high cost of fighting Communism. For the Equadorians too will have suffered a great loss, the governor of Lago Agrio.

CHAPTER 8

The three Americans found Colonel Escobar waiting for them at the main gate of the Ecuadorian Special Forces compound. The man looked every bit the Airborne Ranger Powers had said the colonel to be.

Escobar stood six-four and was 220 pounds of solid muscle. The camouflage uniform he wore looked tailor made and fit perfectly over his muscular frame. Powers had said the man was forty-four, but the deep bronze tan of his handsomely rugged face and the sparkling green eyes made him appear ten years younger. The small black mustache along his upper lip was neatly trimmed.

Greetings and introductions were exchanged. Colonel Escobar then climbed into the jeep next to Captain Jackson and directed their driver to his headquarters building. They went straight to the briefing room where Major Roberto Salazar, Escobar's executive officer, waited for them. Once again introductions were made while a sergeant brought in a pot of coffee and a tray of cups. Filling a cup for each of the officers, the sergeant then left the room. Escobar picked up a cup and took his place at the head of the large teakwood table. The others did the same. Once everyone was seated, Escobar looked over at Mattson. The colonel's voice was deep, and he spoke flawless English.

"Major Mattson, my friend Colonel Powers informed me that you may require my services in dealing with the present situation. Of course, I assume this meeting has to do with the disappearance of Mr. Paul Bracken."

"Yes, sir, it does. That, and possibly an internal security problem within your country."

The last remark brought no visible indication of concern from Escobar.

"Please continue, Major. What exactly can my command and I do for you?"

Mattson spent the next twenty minutes going over the details of the reports they had read and the comments and reactions of those they had spoken with since arriving in the country. He especially made a point of detailing the briefing they had been given by General Parros. He concluded by announcing the pending arrival of the two A-Teams from Panama and the two flight crews due in from MacDill.

"And that's about it, Colonel. We were hoping to use your compound as a central base of operations while trying to locate the guerrillas and sort this thing out."

Escobar sat motionless the entire time. There had been no change in his expression, not even one question, only those penetrating green eyes fixed unwaveringly on Mattson. The room had fallen strangely silent. All were waiting for Escobar to speak. Leaning back in his chair, the colonel interlaced his fingers and brought his hands up, tapping his extended index fingers against his lips, eyes still studying the American major.

A full minute of silence passed before Escobar lowered his hands and said, "You will have to pardon me, gentlemen. I was remembering something I was taught many years ago at your Officer Candidate School in Fort Benning. A major, I believe it was, told us that as officers and leaders we must always demonstrate proper respect and dignity to our fellow officers. For not only were we the epitome of gentlemen, but the honored protectors of our country as well." Escobar paused briefly, as if pondering his next words, then continued. "Unfortunately, General Arturo Parros possesses neither of these fine qualities. To be frank, Major, the man is a thief and a cold-blooded murderer. He would kill his own mother if he felt it would serve his purpose. He is a disgrace to both the uniform and our country. I say this to set your mind to rest, Major Mattson. It is clearly obvious that you feel the general is somehow involved in all of this. I can assure you gentlemen, neither my unit nor I are obligated in any way to General Parros or to any other high ranking officer within the military. We have sworn a blood oath to President Pizarro and to the sovereignty of our country. Major, I can promise you, no one would take greater pleasure in proving that Parros is involved in our current problems. It would give me great pleasure to personally shoot the bastard between the eyes."

Major Salazar struggled to restrain a smile. Jake winked at B.J. from across the table. They had found an ally, and a damned formidable one, at that. Mattson lifted his coffee cup in a salute as he said, "I take it, then, you have no objection to the use of your compound and possibly you and your men."

"Of course not, my friend. We welcome your assistance in dealing with both our problems. Salud!"

Tommy Smith and the two chopper crews flew into Quito on a commercial Eastern Airlines flight and reported directly to Colonel Powers. One hour later, Sergeant Major McMillan and Operation Detachments A-772 and A-776 arrived aboard an unmarked C-130. The plane taxied to an isolated area of the airfield where they and their equipment were loaded onto two buses with blacked out windows.

Assuring that everything was on board, the buses drove out the gates and headed for the Special Forces compound.

Jackson had gone with Major Salazar to make arrangements for incoming personnel. Mattson and Mortimer remained with Escobar to work out a plan for the day's operation. The colonel expressed his concern over possible massive U.S. intervention. Although highly appreciative of the military weapons and training provided by the Americans, he had no great desire to turn over his country's military operations to them. Those were Ecuadorian problems and he felt his country could handle them. Jake and B.J. agreed.

A sergeant came to the door and announced the arrival of the buses from the airport. The three officers went out to meet them. Sergeant Major Kenny McMillan was the first to step out.

The rangy, six-foot SF veteran of nearly thirty years saw B.J. and howled, "Good God! They'll promote any fuckin' body these days, won't they major?"

"Hell yes. They have to, you damn NCOs won't take commissions. Kenny, how are you?" Asked B.J. as the two old friends shook hands.

"Just fine, B.J. Brought you some of the finest hell raisers we've got and they're hot to trot. They look kinda young, but don't let that fool you. They've been around."

The communications officer came over. "Excuse me, Colonel Escobar. President Pizarro is on the line and would like to speak with you."

"Thank you, Captain. Major Mattson, if you will show your men to their quarters, they can store their gear and we will meet in the briefing room in thirty minutes."

"That will be fine, sir. See you in thirty minutes," said B.J. as he saluted the departing colonel.

McMillan watched the Ecuadorian commander walk

away before saying, "Colonel Ramon Escobar, age forty-four—attended Airborne School, Ranger School, SF School, OCS, and the School of the Americas, where he was named the honor graduate. Totally loyal to the government, nearly killed during the last military coup for trying to protect the president and his family. Highly disliked by most of the ranking military brass because he can't be bribed or bought at any price. My kind of guy." The sergeant major smiled.

"Sounds like you did your homework, Sergeant Major," said Jake.

"Always do, sonny, or I mean, sir. Don't think we've ever met."

"Lieutenant Commander Jacob Mortimer, Naval Special Warfare Command, presently assigned to USSOCOM, MacDill. Pleased to meet you."

McMillan shook hands with the naval officer, a smile on his lips. "Mortimer!" McMillan had seen the SEAL patch on the officer's fatigues. "A SEAL named Mortimer. My, my. I won't even get into the implications of that one, sir, although I'm sure I'd hear some interesting stories. Anyway, you'll be happy to know that A-776 is made up of Special Forces Scuba personnel. I'm sure you boys will have a lot to talk about."

Two young captains stepped from the bus. McMillan introduced them. "Major, this is Captain Charlie Cleveland, Commander of ODA-772, and this is Captain James Hay, CO of ODA-776. They and their teams all have ground time in El Salvador, and have worked with DEA in Colombia and Bolivia."

Both officers seemed very young.

"Pleased to meet you, gentlemen. Let's get the teams situated. We have a meeting with Colonel Escobar in about twenty minutes."

McMillan turned and yelled through the door of the bus. "OK, girls! Break time's over. Let's give the American taxpayer his money's worth. Head it up and move it out."

The teams stored their equipment and were back in the briefing room within the allotted time. Colonel Escobar entered and everyone in the room leaped to attention. "Please be seated, gentlemen. I have just been in contact with Senor Juan Pizarro, the president of my country. The attack on the Lago Agrio oilfields last night has caused near panic within the legislative branch of the government. They are calling for massive U.S. assistance. The President has asked me if I thought, with your arrival, we could curtail the need for such drastic action. I asked that we be given forty-eight hours to try. If by that time we are not successful, such action would be warranted. The casualties from last night's attack have left five government soldiers dead and four seriously wounded or burned. I also regret to tell you that five Americans of the Texaco oil crew were killed in that action. And then, of course, there is still the matter of the missing consul general. Major Mattson and Commander Mortimer have studied the map and divided it like so." Turning to the map, Escobar used a pointer to tap the areas that had been marked out in red.

"The two A-Teams will take the two sectors to the east, while I deploy two of the Ecuadorian detachments to the south, and an additional three to the west. Unfortunately, gentlemen, although I have four full companies at my disposal, I can not commit the entire unit. The President has requested that one company be deployed around the capitol to provide the legislators a sense of protection; one company must remain here in case a full scale uprising should occur. And Bravo Company is presently in training at your Airborne School at Fort Benning. That leaves us only one company and forty-eight hours to cover an area roughly three hundred square miles in size."

The number given by Escobar brought a low murmur from the young SF troopers. That three hundred square miles the colonel was talking about was anything but flat ground. They all had experience in moving through South American jungles. Forty-eight hours was the same as no time at all.

Escobar paused to let them consider the difficulty of the operation, then said, "I have arranged to have four UH1H helicopters placed at your disposal. The remaining aircraft will provide transportation and support for my company. Major Salazar and one platoon of the Rapid Deployment Force will be attached to your A-Teams. If you gentlemen will see him after this meeting, you can inform him as to how you would like that force utilized in your operation. Should you find that there is a problem with your communications equipment, please feel free to contact my signal officer. We have a very high level of inventory on hand. Replacement can be arranged. Major, Commander, is there anything I have left out?"

Jake stared across at Mattson and shook his head in the negative.

"No sir. I believe that covers it. The commander and I will answer any other questions the teams may have while we are preparing to launch."

"Very, well then, gentlemen, I wish us all good luck and good hunting."

Escobar laid the pointer down and headed for the door. The men in the room jumped to attention. After the door had shut behind him, the room came alive with excited chatter. Kenny McMillan stepped to the front of the table and yelled, "All right, ladies! If we've got to gossip, let's move our ass over to the team house where we can get some work done at the same time. Move it out."

As the men left the room, Jake called for team leaders and executive officers to remain. The officers turned over the teams to their team sergeants with instructions to have them ready to move in thirty minutes.

Mattson stood at the end of the briefing table and lit a cigarette before he said, "OK, fellows, first off, I want you to know that Commander Mortimer and I are here solely to assist you with intelligence information and to provide advice if you feel you are uncertain about any aspect of this operation. The key thing I'm trying to get across is that these are your teams. You are the team leaders. You have total and absolute control at all times. The commander and I will be going with each team, but at no time will we interfere or question any order given by you or your executive officer. In effect, we are just one of the boys. We will follow whatever orders are given by you. Is this understood? I do not want any man in this room to feel that he is under any type of pressure by our presence. You are in control and I do not expect any of you to make decisions or take actions that you would not normally take if we were not along for the ride. Do I have any questions?"

Captain Hay flipped the ashes from his cigarette in the ashtray before asking, "Major Mattson, besides the kidnapping and the guerrilla activity, Captain Cleveland and I were advised of an internal security problem in the country. I noticed that Colonel Escobar made no reference to such a problem. Could you explain that?"

"Major Salazar, sir, would you care to handle that one?" asked B.J.

Salazar tapped the end of his pencil on the yellow pad in front of him as he looked across the table at the team leaders.

"Yes, Major, thank you. Gentlemen, regrettably, not all military leaders of my country are as dedicated as Colonel Escobar. There is one general in particular that you will soon encounter who would sell this country down the river if he could make enough money from the deal. That man is General Parros. It is in his district that you will be operating. He has established his own private army in the area, and as much as I am shamed by having to say it, neither he nor his men should be trusted. We, Colonel Escobar and I, as well as Major Mattson and the commander, believe that Parros and his men are involved in the events that are shaking our country."

"Excuse me, sir, but do we have any hard evidence to back up that theory?" asked Captain Cleveland.

The question stilled Salazar's pencil tapping. A look of despair crossed the man's face as he said, "I do not know if you could call it, hard evidence, Captain, but it was our unit that had to recover the bodies of Captain Sanchez and the twenty-nine men who died with him. It was not a pleasant experience, I can assure you. The bodies were returned here. It was not until our camp doctor examined the bodies that we discovered a very strange thing. Every man had no fewer than five bullet wounds in his body and each and every one had been caused by a 7.62 round. Does that not seem unusual to you, captain?" asked Salazar.

Cleveland thought about it for a second before he answered. "It would bring up two very interesting questions, Major."

"Which are?"

"One, guerrillas never have an overabundance of ammunition; too hard to come by in their situation. So why use so much on men who were apparently dead already? Second, it is highly unlikely that any guerrilla force in the world is fortunate enough to have a weapons arsenal made up solely of one type of rifle, that fires only one type of ammunition."

Mattson and Mortimer smiled, as did Salazar, at the young captain's answer. "Exactly, Captain," answered Salazar. "But, you see, Captain Sanchez and his men were to be extracted by helicopter. They say when they arrived at the LZ, the men were already dead. One of my sergeants found a number of these scattered over the area of the slaughter." Salazar pulled three brass casings from his shirt pocket and rolled them across the table to Cleveland.

Captain Hay took one in his hand and turned it end over end a couple of times, before saying, "Seven point sixty-two. I bet the next thing you're going to tell us is that the extraction choppers were carrying M-60 machine guns."

"Twin-mounted, both doors," said Salazar.

"Holy shit!" exclaimed Cleveland. "Guess that's about as hard as it gets. They gunned down their own men. And we're going to work with this asshole, Jesus, what a deal."

"That's why I had the two crews from the Special Operations Wing sent down here," said Mattson. "We can't prove anything yet. But that doesn't mean we have to play sitting duck for these people. I figured you men ought to know what you're up against. You have the option of telling your teams what you heard here or keeping it to yourselves. That's your choice. Now, if there are no more questions, I believe we had better get on the stick. Colonel Escobar has bought us forty-eight hours and we can't afford the luxury of wasting any of that time."

While Jake and the others went to the team house, Mattson headed for the communications center to call Powers and update him on the situation. Luckily, Colonel Escobar had managed to convince President Pizarro to give him forty-eight hours before formally requesting U.S.

intervention. B.J. was certain that decision would upset more than a few members of the JCS and the National Security Council, but his decision would take some of the pressure for immediate action off General Johnson and the President, as well as provide them with a little more time to solve the problem. As he waited for Powers to come on the line, Mattson thought of Captain Sanchez and his men. He was convinced that Parros had ordered the action, but he was going to have to prove that. It was that very proof that he intended to get tonight.

No special equipment would be required. Only two bottles of tequila and a few hours alone with Governor Duran.

Colonel Suplao watched as the last case of rifles and ammunition were lowered into the trench. While the guerrillas filled in the hole, Suplao noted the coordinates in a small black notebook and placed it in his shirt pocket. All the weapons and ammo, as well as the names and records of the supporters of the revolution, had been hidden and their location noted. Although this planned revolution had temporarily been halted, the tools required to begin again would always remain.

Major Ochoa and Carlos Cruz had organized what was left of their army. Of the nearly six hundred they had begun with, only two hundred remained. Colonel Suplao had gone from group to group and explained the necessity for withdrawal. As he had expected, a number of the Ecuadorian guerrillas saw this only as a ploy by the Cubans to abandon their cause. For them the countless hours of training and political education had been for nothing. Disheartened and bitter, they chose to leave. Others accepted the situation, but preferred to remain in their country to be with their families. They would be ready to begin again when the Cubans returned. The remainder had elected to go back to Nicaragua, where they would receive more training, and await the time for a new revolution.

Conducting one final inspection of the cache sites, Suplao called his officers together and briefed them on the routes they were to take in their movement from the mountains across the Putumayo River into Colombia. Colonel Suplao and two of the Cuban officers would depart first with one hundred of the men broken down into two groups of fifty each. They would travel north-northeast until they crossed the river, then swing west to Puerto Asis.

Ochoa, Cruz, and the remaining two Cuban commanders would depart the camp two hours behind the lead element, go directly north and straight across the river. They would regroup and link up with the Colombian guerrillas to the west of Puerto Asis.

Suplao had asked if there were any questions, there had been none. Satisfied that all signs of the former base camp had been erased, he bade his fellow officers good-bye. Moving to the head of the first column he gave the order to move out. Ochoa watched until the last man of the first group disappeared into the thick jungle. They were on their way. Soon they would be home again.

Cruz stood by Ochoa's side and watched the departure. "The coronel seemed saddened because we are having to leave," he said.

Ochoa lowered his head. He knew he had been the cause of this failure. Fidel would have many questions when they returned. But it would be Colonel Suplao who would suffer Castro's wrath, not Ochoa. He knew Suplao well. The man would take the blame for all that had gone wrong here, just as Ochoa's father had taken the blame for a young Captain Suplao's mistakes at the Bay of Pigs, so many years ago.

• • •

General Parros stood on the balcony of his headquarters and watched the long line of helicopters as they circled the compound and landed in the vast open field beyond the main gates. The Special Forces teams were finally here. Colonel Rivas joined the general on the balcony and informed him that all had gone well with the movement of the consul general. Bracken was on Genovesa, under the protection of a platoon of commandos. Radio communications had been established and the platoon would await further orders.

Parros smiled his approval at the news, but the smile quickly faded as he saw the men unloading from the first two choppers. The bright green berets of the Americans were intermingled with the powder blue berets of Colonel Escobar's elite Special Forces. Rivas stepped forward and leaned on the wrought iron railing along the front of the balcony. They had not expected the Americans to join forces with Escobar. There were few people in this country that Rivas feared, but next to the general himself Colonel Escobar was second on that list.

Turning to Parros, Rivas tried to hide the concern in his face, but a shaky voice gave him away. "General. This—this changes everything. We had planned only to ambush and kill the twenty-five or thirty American advisors. But, now—now that Colonel Escobar has committed his men to the American major, we—can't possibly—I mean, my God! Ramon Escobar will go crazy if we do this thing. We must devise another plan."

Parros remained calm as he listened to Rivas, watching four more of the helicopters land. Two of them unloaded their cargo and lifted off again to return to Quito. Mattson, Mortimer, Jackson, and Escobar were coming through the gates when he turned to Rivas and asked, "Why would this new development change our plans, Colonel?"

"Sir, you know how close the President is to Escobar. Escobar will not stop until he has found those responsible for the killing of these men."

"So? Let him go find the guerrillas who committed the act. That only makes it easier for us. We also want to rid the country of the guerrillas, don't we, Colonel Rivas?"

"Why, yes, sir. But—"

"Colonel, you overrate this so-called Ecuadorian Rambo. If your men should be lucky enough to get him in their sights, so much the better. We will need to make only one change. You will have to increase the number of men in the ambush party by at least twenty, I would say. No, on second thought, let's make that fifty, just to be sure. Are your men ready?"

Rivas realized that arguing further with Parros would do no good.

"Yes, sir, I will add fifty more. That will give me close to one hundred men. Three Chinook helicopters are standing by at their location. Once the Americans have briefed you on where they plan to begin their search, and I have received the coordinates by radio for those areas, the chinooks will transport my men to those locations and they will select an ambush site."

"What of the two gunships?" asked Parros.

"They will converge on the area once the ambush has been initiated and make multiple passes until they have suppressed the Americans' fire. My men will then move forward and finish off any survivors."

"Outstanding, Colonel. So you see, there is no real problem here. We will only need to use a few more bullets, that is all," laughed Parros.

The general was still laughing as the Americans and

Escobar came into the room. Parros put on a great act of welcoming Colonel Escobar, but only a blind man could miss the look of pure hate that showed on Escobar's face.

Ignoring Escobar's refusal to shake his hand, Parros wasted no time in moving the group to the briefing room. Colonel Rivas excused himself as he had other pressing matters needing his attention. Once everyone was seated, Parros began by welcoming Colonel Escobar and his men as well as the American A-Teams. If they were now ready, he was prepared to receive a briefing on their plan of operation for the day.

Mattson nodded for Cleveland and Hay to begin. The two SF captains walked to the front of the room and placed a large map of the area on the wall. Cleveland presented the operations plan while Captain Hay pointed out the areas where the search would begin on the map. Both officers had gone to Mattson before departing Quito. They were concerned that if Parros was the man behind the murder of Captain Sanchez, that briefing him on their every move could place them in the same situation. Could they forego the briefing for Parros? Mattson had told them it had to be done. If they didn't present a plan of operation to the general, they would be leaving themselves wide open for an "accidental air strike or artillery barrage." Parros could justify that by simply stating that they had not presented a detailed operations plan and he had no idea they were in the area when he had ordered the strike. Neither officer had liked the answer, but realized there was little they could do about it. It was rather like playing Russian roulette with a fully loaded gun.

By the time Cleveland finished, Parros had all the information he needed. Standing, he praised the young SF captain for his attention to detail and the professional manner in which they had planned the operation. He then introduced his communications officer. He would provide frequencies and call signs for the provincial command. As the officer stepped to the podium, Parros smoothed down his mustache with his fingers. This was a prearranged signal for the guard at the door to come forward and inform the general that he had an urgent phone call. This done, Parros excused himself from the briefing and left the room. Within minutes, Colonel Rivas's commandos had the exact coordinates of where the Americans intended to land, and their direction of march. Returning to the briefing room, Parros went directly to his seat next to Mortimer. As he sat down, Jake whispered, "I hope the call wasn't anything serious, General."

"No, not at all, Commander," smiled Parros. "Only a minor problem, but one that can be taken care of quite easily."

The communications officer concluded his portion of the briefing and turned it back over to Parros. The general stepped behind the podium and, smiling broadly, said, "Gentlemen, I believe that concludes this briefing. As pointed out earlier, you have call signs for our tactical air support as well as the artillery. My men will be waiting to serve you, should it become necessary. Let's hope that shall not be required. As Colonel Escobar has requested that my troops not accompany this operation, I shall nevertheless maintain them on a standby condition, should they be needed. Now, if there are no more questions of me or my staff, I wish you a safe journey and a successful mission."

All but Colonel Escobar rose to their feet as the general departed the room.

"Boy, if this guy is as dirty as you guys think he is, he's got one hell of a smooth act there," remarked Captain Jim Hay. It was the same thing everyone in the room was thinking. Everyone except Escobar.

As the teams made their way to the waiting helicopters, Jake asked Mattson, "Hey, B.J., what happened to the guys from MacDill? I thought Master Sergeant Smith was supposed to come in with two flight crews?"

"He did. They're with Colonel Powers at the embassy. I've got to call them right now. You go ahead and check out the load plan for the insertion with our two Captains."

Jake nodded and went through the gates while Mattson went to the communications shack. The officer on duty showed him to the phone and, surprisingly, left the room. B.J. figured someone would be monitoring his call. Powers came on the line.

"Good morning, Major. How is it going so far?" he asked.

"Not bad, sir. We expect to be airborne and begin insertions within the next thirty minutes. Anything from Q-Tip?"

"Yes, just a few minutes ago. He doesn't know how you did it, but he said to thank you for the extra time. The brass was sure Pizarro would request immediate intervention after the oil business last night. When he told 'em he wanted to wait forty-eight hours, Q-Tip said you could hear the crying all the way to Florida, and it damn near gave your boy Sweet a heart attack. Blood pressure went off the scale. J.J. filled the President in on what's going on down here. The man is worried about Bracken, but he's just as worried about you guys. Said to be sure to tell you to keep your ass down."

"The President of the United States said that?"

"Sure enough. Remember this guy's been in the shit before; he knows what it's like."

"Thank God for that! Colonel, is Sergeant Smith anywhere handy? I need to speak to him for a minute."

"He's right here, Major. Just a moment."

Smith came on the line in his usual jubilant mood.

"Hey there, Major. How's it hangin'? Thought there for a while you'd just brought me and the boys down here for a little R and R in the local bars. You know how them fly boys love Latin women. What can I do for ya?"

"Smitty, do you remember that jerry-rigging we saw on the birds when we were in Bolta Land last year?"

"Sure. The land of the big apartheid. You talkin' about the mounted—" Smith suddenly stopped talking. He had been around this business long enough to realize that Mattson had a reason for not just saying what he meant. Someone must be eavesdropping on Ma Bell. "Uh–yeah, I sure do. Worked out real well a few days later, if I remember right."

"That's right, Smitty. Well, look, we may need something along that line before the day is over. Let Powers know what you need. He'll see you get it. As soon as the baby is ready to burp, pick her up and take her for a walk. Keep your walkman tuned to KFLA FM; they could be playing the blues before long. You got it, Smitty?"

"Loud and clear, Major. Anything else?"

"Yeah, you might want to watch yourself when you go for that walk. There's some pretty tough kids on the block. The baby-sitter is suspected of child abuse," said Mattson.

"Do tell. Well, we'll just have to see if we can't provide a little counseling for that problem."

"Guess that's it, Smitty. Be talking to you later. So long."

Mattson hung up the phone. As he was leaving the building, he noticed the confused look on the commo officer's face. Smiling at him, B.J. asked, in perfect Spanish, "Trouble with the kids, Captain?"

The question left a totally bewildered man even more confused, as he watched the major go out the door laughing.

CHAPTER 9

The four lead helicopters carried Mortimer and the two A-teams. Four other choppers followed with thirty-two of Colonel Escobar's men aboard. They were to be set down on the LZ with the Americans, and the choppers would return to the SF compound to ferry the colonel and the rest of his men into the western sector. B.J. had made sure that General Parros had seen him board the lead chopper with Mortimer. Once out of sight of Parros's headquarters, the helicopter touched down outside of town and Major Mattson, Major Salazar, and Captain Jackson leaped out. The chopper then lifted off and joined the others, heading for the eastern mountains.

This part of the operation had not been included in Captain Cleveland's briefing. Both Mattson and Escobar were certain that Governor Duran was somehow linked to Parros and the disappearance of Bracken. They would never be able to get anything out of the man in the presence of Parros or Colonel Rivas, but alone, and with the help of the tequila, Mattson figured they had a chance. Major Salazar had been sent along by Escobar in case there was trouble with the guards, and to officially arrest the governor if their theory proved to be true. B.J. informed Salazar that he would try the diplomatic approach first, but if that didn't appear to be getting them anywhere, he was going to have to get rough. That seemed to delight the Ecuadorian major. Captain Jackson had been brought along simply because B.J. didn't think the young officer had enough experience to be slugging it out in the jungles with hard core guerrillas. Besides, he liked the kid, and didn't want to see him get hurt if he could help it.

A jeep and driver were waiting for them as they walked the short distance to the main road into town. Once seated in the jeep, Salazar instructed the driver to head for the governor's estate. All three men checked their side arms to make sure they had a round in the chamber. The only thing about a sure plan was the fact that there was no such thing. Mattson had learned long ago to never underestimate his enemies.

As the jeep pulled to a stop at the wrought iron gates at the front entrance, a captain came out. Seeing the two majors, he saluted smartly. All three men noticed the white skull on the officer's shoulder patch. Parros had replaced the regular troops with those of his own. The captain asked what their business was with the governor. Colonel Escobar had foreseen the probability of this happening and prepared a false document that Salazar now presented to the officer on duty. It stated that the three men were to remain with the governor for the next twenty-four hours and not let the man out of their sight. The signature was an excellent forgery of General Arturo Parros.

The captain recognized the general's signature, handed the paper back to Salazar, and waved to the guards to open the gates. Mattson breathed a sigh of relief. So far, so good. More soldiers were sitting on the steps in front of the mansion. As the jeep pulled up, they stood to attention and saluted the officers as they stepped from the vehicle, went up the stairs, and inside. One of Parros's men came over to the driver and asked for a light for his cigarette. The young Ecuadorian Special Forces soldier obliged. Sticking the lighter back in his pocket, he shifted slightly in the seat, and, without making any sudden move, flipped the safety switch off on the Israeli Uzi next to his left leg. His instructions had been simple. If he heard gunfire in the house he was to kill the men on the steps.

Two burly bodyguards flanked the entrance to the study, their eyes fixed on the approaching officers, their hands behind their backs and on Mac-10 machine pistols attached to their belts. Salazar presented the paper again. Finding it satisfactory, one of the men opened the door for them. Duran had passed out at the bar. An empty tequila bottle teetered precariously on the edge of the bar. The bodyguard shook his head and remarked that the man had been drinking all day, then went out, closing the door behind him. Mattson moved quickly to check on Duran, while Salazar went into the bathroom and wet down a towel with ice cold water. Returning to the bar, he asked Mattson, "How is he?"

"Soaked to the gills. It's a wonder the son of a bitch isn't dead from alcohol poisoning."

They moved him from the bar to a large chair in the corner of the room and Salazar began wiping his face with the cold rag. At first it seemed to have no effect. Then, gradually, Duran began to moan and slap out at the annoying wetness he now felt on his face.

"Jackson, go in that bathroom and see what you can find that will make this guy puke his guts out," said Mattson.

Salazar went for another wet rag while Jackson returned with a bottle of castor oil and a bottle of cherry flavored Vicks 44 cough medicine.

"Which one do you want to try?" he asked.

"Get a glass and mix them together. That should go real well with the tequila," answered B.J. Jackson nearly got sick thinking about it as he went to the bar and poured the two in a glass and brought it back to Mattson.

Salazar saw the concoction and threw the rag away. Pulling Duran's head back, he held the man's chin so that Mattson could pour the mix down the governor's throat. Duran almost gagged before the glass was empty. His bloodshot eyes fluttered open as he coughed, spitting half the contents in his mouth all over the front of B.J.'s shirt. "Shit!" whispered Mattson as he continued to force the rest of the stuff down Duran's throat.

Within seconds after the glass was empty, Duran's face began to turn a beet red and he began to heave. Salazar and Mattson grabbed him under his arms and half ran, half dragged the man into the bathroom. Getting him to the sink just in time. Five minutes later, so weak from the vomiting that they had to hold him up, Duran begged to sit down. They carried him back to the chair, and stood over him.

Struggling to focus his watery eyes, Duran asked, "What—What are you people doing here? How did you— get in here? You can't just walk in any time you please. I'm—I'm the governor, Goddamn it! Get out! Get out, all of you. I'm a powerful man—yes—a powerful man." Duran's voice began to trail off. "I'm—I'm the governor—"

Salazar looked down at the pale, sweat drenched face of Miguel Duran. For a fleeting moment he felt a spark of pity for the man. What could he have been, had he not become involved with a man like Parros? Now no one, not even Duran himself, would ever know.

Mattson reached out and, gripping the front of the man's shirt, pulled him forward in the chair. "Wake up, Duran. Wake up! Listen to me. We know you are involved with General Parros. Tell us what we want to know and we may be able to help you. Can you hear me, Duran?" Shaking the half unconscious man, B.J. was losing patience. "Goddamn it, Duran! You're going to talk to me whether you want to or not! Jackson, help me get this bastard into the shower. I'll either sober him up, or drown his fucking ass."

Placing him on the floor in the corner of the shower, Mattson adjusted the shower head and turned the cold water on full blast. Duran moaned and tried to crawl away from the freezing water. B.J. kept the shower head directly on him, refusing to let him escape the downpour.

Outside, Salazar's driver saw two cars approaching in his side view mirror. He watched them make their way up the circle drive and park behind his jeep. The windows were tinted so he could not tell who was inside. He waited for someone to get out. No one did. One of the guards walked down the steps and to the driver's side of the first car. The window was lowered only inches as the guard leaned forward. From his vantage point by the mirror the SF driver could see the man was talking to someone in the car. He was too far away to hear what was being said. The guard straightened up, then called another guard to the car. Both men spoke for a moment then walked back up to the jeep. The same man who had asked for a light earlier asked for another. Moving his hand from the Uzi, the young driver pulled the lighter from his pocket and held it out to the guard. Placing a cigarette in his mouth, the man smiled and reached forward as if to take the lighter. Instead, he grabbed the driver's wrist and jerked him forward against the steering wheel. The boy started to yell, but before he could, the second guard placed his hand over his mouth and at the same time pulled the man's head back and cut his throat.

The doors of the two cars opened and Colonel Rivas, along with six of his men, stepped out. They were dressed in solid black commando uniforms. The black stocking masks had been turned up and rested on their foreheads. The two guards shoved the still quivering body of the driver onto the passenger side, placed the jeep in neutral, and quietly pushed it away from the front of the house. Rivas signaled three of his men to enter through the front. He and the other three were to circle around and go through the French doors that led to the room next to the study. The guards had been his men, but the bodyguards were loyal only to Duran. They would have to be killed. Rivas had insisted on the mask as a precaution. It was highly unlikely that anyone in the house would get out alive, but if they should, they would not be able to identify anyone.

Pulling their masks down and in place, the would-be assassins locked their silencers onto their weapons and moved up the steps in front of the house while Rivas and the others disappeared into the hedges and worked their way along the west side of the mansion.

Duran sat shivering in the chair, his soaked clothes dripping puddles of water in a circle around him. He stared glassy-eyed at Mattson and Salazar. Although still feeling sick, he had recovered enough to realize what was happening to him. Salazar stood in front of him, hands on his hips, awaiting an answer to his question about General Parros. The American major and the captain sat at the bar, also awaiting his answer. He did not know how much they knew, but it really didn't matter anymore. Once Parros found out they had been here, he would be a dead man.

"I will ask you only once more, Governor. Was General Parros involved in the killing of Captain Sanchez and his men?" demanded Salazar.

"Ye—Yes. He was. It was his plan to—"

Duran stopped in mid sentence as a series of muffled sounds echoed in the hall, followed by a loud thud, as something fell against the door. Mattson and Salazar recognized the sounds immediately. Pulling their pistols, they both dived for cover. Jackson wasn't sure what was happening, but the sight of the guns told him it wasn't anything good. He flung himself behind the bar with Mattson. Duran was trying to will his body to move, but he couldn't. Salazar reached around the chair and tried to pull the man down, but there wasn't time. The double oak doors flew open and a hail of automatic weapons fire from three 9mm machine guns raked the room.

Glasses shattered and wood splintered as bullets tore apart the teakwood bar. Salazar fell to the floor to the left of the chair and fired four rapid rounds from his Beretta, three of the slugs catching one of the men square in the chest and catapulting him back out into the hallway.

Mattson nodded to the far end of the bar, then pointed to his end. They would swing around the ends and fire at the same time. Jackson nodded that he understood. "Now!" yelled B.J.

Mattson's first round went wide, but the second and third caught his target in the head. Blood and brains splattered the oak doors. Jackson's proficiency with a 9mm Beretta was about as good as his Spanish. Two rounds went in the floor, a third hit his man in the foot, the fourth in the arm and a fifth in the hand. Salazar and Mattson both zeroed in on the man and finally put him out of his misery, before Jackson could shoot him apart, one piece at a time.

The heavy smell of cordite hung over the room as the three men slowly stood and moved cautiously toward the dead man. Salazar went to each body and removed the mask. The third one he removed sent a shock wave through him.

"Major! That's the soldier guarding the door at the

briefing. Remember? He came and told the general he had an urgent call."

B.J. didn't answer; he bent over and picked up one of the silenced weapons and turned to Salazar. "Guess we've got our answers now."

Before the major could answer, the side doors to the study burst open and the shattering hammer of automatic weapons fire again filled the room. This time they were not as lucky. Jackson managed to get off two shots before a burst from the men in black tore through his leg and side, knocking him to the floor. Mattson nailed one of the assassins in the gut with three rounds from the Uzi before diving behind a couch only seconds ahead of a fusillade of bullets that ripped through the wood and fabric inches above his head. Hugging the floor, he tried to crawl to the end of the couch, when suddenly something hit him in the head. The room seemed to go a deep orange before the lights went out.

Salazar stood flat footed and, ignoring the hail of bullets tearing the wall behind him apart, he gripped the pistol with both hands, and taking careful aim, shot one of the men through the head and another through the heart. Swinging the pistol onto the last man, he pulled the trigger. There was a loud click, as the hammer fell on an empty chamber. Salazar was out of bullets.

The man in black paused for a second with his MP-5 leveled at Salazar, as if wanting to enjoy the moment. The major lowered his pistol to his side and let it fall to the floor. The man took a step closer and whispered, "Perhaps if you beg hard enough, I will let you live."

Salazar spat at the man's feet and smiled as he answered, "Fuck you!"

The first bullet passed cleanly through Salazar's heart; he never felt the other thirteen that ripped his body apart. The man in black stood over him and added a final shot to the head, then whispered, "Fuck you, amigo." Turning to the body of Captain Jackson, he could see he was still alive. Changing magazines, he chambered a round and was about to shoot the young captain in the head, when he heard a moan from behind the couch. The American major was still alive. Forgetting about the captain for the moment, he walked around the end of the couch and stared down at Mattson. Blood covered the left side of his head. It had been a near miss. A fraction of an inch more and his skull would have been plastered on the wall.

Focusing his blurry eyes on the figure standing above him, B.J. knew it was over. Still half dazed, he heard the man say, "Too bad you came all this way to die, gringo."

Mattson's head hurt and he didn't feel like listening to a bunch of horseshit. "Well, do it, you sorry sack of shit. Or are you gonna talk me to death?"

"As you wish, gringo."

Two loud shots rang out. B.J.'s body went tense, expecting to feel the hot lead tear through him. But there was no pain. Looking up, he saw the man pitch forward into the wall and slide to the floor. Grabbing up the MP-5, Mattson slowly peered over the couch. Standing in the doorway was a tall blond American with a .357 magnum in his hand.

"Woah, Major. I'm on your side. It's OK. That was the last one. The rest of 'em are out of the game."

Pulling himself up, B.J. staggered slightly and gripped the couch to steady his weak knees. "Mister Highfield, I presume," he said.

Replacing the magnum in its shoulder holster, he came across the room and helped Mattson to a chair as he replied, "The one and only. And you must be Major B.J. Mattson."

"Yeah. What the hell are you doing here? I figured the

Agency would have gotten you out of the country on the first thing leaving the ground."

Highfield knelt by Jackson. Pulling one of the masks from the dead man next to him, he tied it around the captain's leg and checked the wound in the side as he said, "Oh, they did. I just wasn't ready to leave yet. Know what I mean? Just didn't figure I could fuck up and then leave without making things right. Shit, Major, that don't exactly help your resume, you know. Your captain here is going to be all right, but Major Salazar's had it. Same with the gov there."

Mattson said, "What—Where—" Looking down beside the chair, B.J. saw Duran sprawled on the floor. Four neat little holes surrounded by blood stains lined the front of his white silk shirt.

"Shit!" said Mattson. "We needed that bastard alive to testify against General Parros."

"Not necessarily, Major."

"What are you talking about, secret agent man?"

Highfield picked up a half empty bottle of tequila that lay next to Duran's body and sat down on the floor next to Mattson. Taking a long drink he passed it over to B.J.

"Well, you see, Major, like I said, I can't stand leaving a job half ass done. So I started thinking about some of the conversations Paul Bracken and I used to have. He always thought that fat ass Garces was a crook and he was sure he was linked with Duran and Parros, but he could never prove it. I guess I should have figured it out sooner, but when they snatched Paul, I went a little nuts. I kinda like the old bastard, you know. He's a regular party animal. Anyway. After I got my head on straight, I thought it all out and came up with the idea that the only thing that could possibly link Parros with Garces would have to be money. Since he was the finance minister, the place to start was his office, so I pulled a Watergate. I broke into the ministry and used my computer science degree for something besides a door stop. Accessed the fat man's files and tapes."

Taking a hit off the bottle, B.J. passed it back to Highfield, as he asked, "Did you do any good?"

Pulling a notebook from his shirt pocket, he smiled. "Bingo! This little book names names, account numbers, and amounts. Damn near everybody that's anybody in this town is in here. We're talking millions of dollars here, Major."

"General Parros?"

"Top of the list. Him, Rivas, and Duran."

"We better get that book out of here, then. If Parros finds—"

"Relax, Major. Soon as I hit pay dirt, I punched up a computer printout, ran off two copies, and secured the disk and the notes. Took them straight to President Pizarro's office. Some of Colonel Escobar's boys were on duty there. He gave me a few of them and told me I could have the honor of arresting our ventilated governor there. Him and any of Parros's men that we might find on the premises. We had just disarmed the boys at the main gate when we heard the shoot-out start up at the house. Wish we could have gotten here sooner, but we ran into a few more of Parros's men between the gate and the house."

Mattson leaned forward and slapped the CIA man on the back.

"Mike, I'm just glad you got here when you did. The barrel of that Uzi I was staring at looked like a fucking cannon."

A low moan rose from the man Highfield had shot. Getting to their feet, both men walked around the couch. The man in black had pushed himself up into a sitting position against the wall. A pool of blood was slowly spreading beneath him.

"Well, I'll be damned. I better retire from this business. The day I can't kill a guy with a magnum from forty feet it's time to hang it up."

Mattson knelt beside the dying man and removed his mask. It was Colonel Rivas. Small beads of perspiration made their way down his tortured face. B.J. started to raise his shirt to check the wounds, but Rivas stopped him.

"No—no need, Major Mattson. I—I am a dead man."

Highfield now knelt down next to Rivas. "Colonel, you're one hard son of a bitch. I'll give you that."

"Rivas, we know everything. We've got all the evidence we need to put a rope around the general's neck, so there is no need for you to protect him any more. Tell us. Did he plan the abduction of Bracken?"

Rivas grimaced in pain as his lifeblood slowly leaked out into the floor and he tried to answer. "No—The guerrillas—did—that. But they realized—their mistake and were—were going to return him— Sanchez found—found him. General ordered them killed—needed to destroy—finance ministry—I—" Rivas gasped, then coughed violently. Blood spewed from his mouth.

Mattson knew the man was within seconds of dying. "Rivas! Rivas. Where is Paul Bracken?" Leaning close to the dying man's ear he asked again. "Where is Paul Bracken?"

The colonel coughed again, then his eyes began to roll back. The body jerked once as he whispered, "Geno—Genovesa," then died.

Taking another shot from the bottle, Highfield sat staring at the dead man, repeating the word a couple of times to himself.

"Genovesa. I've heard that name somewhere before."

"I have, too; I just can't remember where."

The sound of sirens made their way into the study as ambulances, police, and soldiers arrived out front. Medics with stretchers came down the hall and Captain Jackson was carefully lifted onto one and rushed back outside. Highfield saw his boss, Rick Hendricks, come into the room. Spotting Highfield, he was all smiles as he came across the room and said, "Great job, Mike. President Pizarro himself called me. You'll be getting a promotion for this."

Finishing off the bottle, Highfield tossed it on the couch. "Yeah, right. Well we ain't done with this thing yet. We still don't have Paul back. Rivas gave us a name before he died. Place called Genovesa. Ever hear of it?"

Hendricks repeated the name a few times, then smiled. "Yes. It's a little island out in the Galapagos chain. One of the few that actually has anything growing on it. Is that where they have Bracken?"

"We think so," said B.J. "What's the President planning to do about Parros?"

"He's already trying to reach Colonel Escobar. Parros has retreated to his ranch outside the town. We figure he's going to fight it out. He knows he's as good as dead anyway. Not going to be an easy job getting him out of there, either. We figure he's got close to three hundred troops that will stand with him. We think he's relying on the other generals in the military coming to his aid, like they did in the last coup."

"Any chance of that?" asked Mattson.

"No way. Any of them that might have considered it have already heard about that book Mike has. They're scooting in all directions to get out of the country before Pizarro has them arrested."

"Have you heard anything from Commander Mortimer, or the A-Teams?"

"Checked with Powers before I came out. The last they

heard they were on the LZ and beginning their sweep. But here's something you might find interesting. Our man in Nicaragua reported a freighter with close to five hundred guerrillas left there a couple of days ago. We believed they were headed here. This morning we picked up a transmission from Cuba. The freighter was ordered to turn back for Nicaragua."

"It would appear that Fidel is trying to back out of this one," said B.J.

Before Hendricks could reply, Colonel Powers burst into the room.

"Major! Our boys are in some deep shit!"

CHAPTER 10

Jake Mortimer leaped, hit the ground, and rolled behind the cover of the rock pile just as a volley of rounds tore the dirt around him. Captain Cleveland hadn't been as lucky. Regaining his footing, he had only been a few feet short of cover when a grenade came rolling down the hill and exploded in front of him. The shrapnel ripped through him like a hot knife through butter, blowing him six feet backward and flat on his back in the open. Sergeant Major McMillan yelled for covering fire and dashed from the trees to the Captain's side. He had hooked him under one arm when he, himself, became engulfed in a hail of bullets that tore him to pieces. As the dust around them cleared, it was apparent that both men were dead.

The sound of rifle fire and exploding grenades was deafening, as Jake reloaded another magazine into his AR-15 automatic rifle and began squeezing off a series of short bursts along the heavily forested hillside. He still hadn't seen who was firing at them, only the muzzle flashes which seemed endless along the ridge. Three bullets ricocheted off the rocks only inches from his head, driving Mortimer back down into the cover of the rocks. He didn't know who they were, but they sure as hell could shoot.

Captain Hay made a rush for the rocks, spraying his entire magazine of thirty rounds into the hill as he ran. Jake watched anxiously as the A-Team commander ran a deadly race against the steady line of bullets that were chewing up the earth behind, hot on his heels. In one desperate leap, he hurled himself into the air, hit the ground hard, and rolled into Mortimer.

"You cut that pretty close, Captain."

Hay's face was covered in dirt and sweat, his breathing heavy, as he replied, "Too fucking close for government work."

"Captain Cleveland and the sergeant major bought it," said Jake.

"Yeah, I know. Seen'em go down hard. We're in a fine fucking mess here; you know that don't you, Commander? We don't get some damn support, we can kiss our ass good-bye."

He didn't have to tell Jake that. All he had to do was look around him. They had off loaded at the LZ with a total of fifty-seven people. Jake, the Two A-Teams, and thirty-two of Escobar's boys. Everything had gone just fine for the first ten minutes, then all hell had broken loose. It had been a textbook ambush. They let the point element walk through, then hit the bulk of the unit right in the middle and closed both front and back doors on them. Jake and the boys were boxed in, and boxed in tight. Of the fifty-seven who had walked into this hell, twenty-one were already dead or wounded. Besides Cleveland and McMillan, four other Green Berets lay dead at the base of the hill. Both Ecuadorian commanders were dead and Captain Cleveland's executive officer had taken command of the Ecuadorian Special Forces unit. The young warrant officer moved along the line, giving encouragement to the foreign SF troops.

"Were you able to make radio contact with anyone, Captain Hay?" asked Jake.

"We tried that base frequency they gave us, but nobody'll answer. Guess we should have figured on that. Given the situation with General Parros, it's not surprising. Sergeant Jones, my commo man, did get through to one of the elements working with Colonel Escobar, but I don't know how much of it they got." Pointing to one of the four bodies by the hill, he said, "The fuckers blew the radio clear through Jonesy's chest."

"What about the other radio?"

"It's lying right out there, Commander," said Hay, pointing to the open ground next the sergeant major's body, "but it might as well be lying a mile away. Anybody that goes for it is going to be staying out there with Charlie and the sergeant major."

Cleveland's executive officer must have had the same idea, but figured he could beat the odds. Having the Ecuadorians lay down a base of cover fire, he made a run for the radio. For a second it looked as if he would make it. Moving at a dead run, he bent and snatched it by the carrying handle, took two steps then stiffened as small puffs of dust flew and the front of his shirt seemed to jump out from his chest three times. He pitched forward and fell face first into the dirt, three bullet holes in his back.

"Goddamn it!" yelled Jake, as he raised up and fired his entire magazine at the hill in frustration. "Come on motherfuckers! You ballless shits! Come on out and fight like fucking men!"

Jake's frustration only served to bring a wrath of bullets in on them.

"Hey, Commander! Next time you start to do that, let me know, will you? I'd like to put in a change of address," said Hay.

Two more Ecuadorians were picked off, and another Green Beret wounded in the next two minutes. They had to get out of this box, or they were all dead. Measuring the volume of fire coming from all around them, Jake and Hay tried to spot the weakest point in the ambush. Right now, it looked like it was the east side. The firing they were receiving from that position had become sporadic. Mortimer would take half of the men who were still able to fight and shoot their way out on that side, then try to flank the shooters on the hillside. If they were lucky, maybe they could break up the ambush. Hay and the remainder of the men would stay with the wounded and provide supporting fire.

Screaming to get the attention of the others around them, Jake pointed to those he wanted to follow him, then to the east position. They signaled that they understood. Locking a fresh magazine in place, he positioned his weight on his push off foot, then yelled, "Now! GO! GO! GO!" They broke for the east ridge, putting out a devastating fire that consumed the men who had been firing on them. Parros's men broke from their cover to the east and tried to escape the wild-eyed, screaming horde that came straight at them. They were easy targets for Jake's assault force. One after another they were knocked over like bowling pins, screaming in pain and rolling lifeless down the side of the hill.

Overrunning the position, Jake halted what was left of his meager force to allow them to catch their breaths. He had lost four more men in the attack.

Hay quickly took advantage of the breathing room and moved his wounded and what was left of his ragged force to the rock strewn formation at the base of the east slope. Now that Jake could cover their back, they only had three directions of fire to worry about.

Jake's heart was pounding wildly as he fought to catch his

breath. He was in great shape, but the Ecuadorian altitude and the rush of adrenaline had taken its toll. One of the Ecuadorian troopers pulled a body from the bushes and, yelling to Mortimer, he pointed to the skull patch on the uniform. In that second, Jake swore to himself that he was going to get out of this thing alive, just so he could have the pleasure of strangling General Parros with his bare hands.

Telling his troops to reload, Mortimer prepared to begin the flanking movement when they heard the sound of approaching helicopters. Captain Hay and his men heard them, too. A loud cheer went up from the Ecuadorians. It was Escobar; he had come to save them. Jake didn't seem as sure. Parros's men were still firing and showing no signs that they feared the approaching birds of prey. Suddenly two gunships appeared above the hill and roared over the battle. All firing stopped as eyes went skyward. Hay gave the thumbs up to Jake and his men as the ships swung wide left and prepared to make their first gun run. Glancing at the body of the man with skull patch, Jake suddenly realized why Parros's men hadn't run. He tried to yell a warning to Hay, but it was too late.

The first gunship unleashed a barrage of 3.7 rockets into Hay's position, then opened up with machine guns. Jake's men flattened themselves against the ground as they caught the tail end of the attack. The second bird swooped in and laid down another barrage of rocket and machine gun fire, then pulled up and out to prepare for another run.

Jake wiped the dirt and dust from his face as he stared down at the dead and dying at the base of the hill. Captain Hay lay in a clearing, both legs and part of his head blown away. Bodies littered the small area. A wounded Ecuadorian tried to get to his feet. The move drew a hail of gunfire from Parros's men on the far hill. Mortimer watched helplessly as bullets slammed into the man repeatedly, even after his lifeless body had fallen to the ground.

Jake and his men tried desperately to dig down into the hard dirt with their bare hands. They were going to be next.

The gunships lined up for their second run. Rockets armed and ready, the first ship tipped its nose down and accelerated. Jake stared up at the death machine as it grew in size and waited for the end to come. Then something unexpected happened. One minute the chopper was there, the next minute it had turned into a massive fireball. The tremendous explosion of fuel, rockets, and bullets, shook the very ground beneath them. Pieces of fiery metal rained down on Parros's troops to the west. Jake was trying to sort out what had happened. His first thought was that a misfire by one of the rockets had destroyed the ship, or a lucky round from one of the men still firing. It had been neither.

The second gunship pulled out of its run when it saw its sister go up in smoke. Now Jake and the others saw why. Two more choppers were in hot pursuit of the gunship. They had U.S. markings on the side.

Tommy Smith double jacked the arming handle on "baby" twin-mounted .50 caliber machine guns, specially installed to limit vibration and provide maximum fire power. Smith was yelling instructions into his throat mike, "Lead him left, Goddamn it, left!"

Pressing down on the twin triggers, Smith arched the tracers right in front of the gunship and tried to catch it in the main blast before he could dive, but he missed. The second U.S. chopper took on the target. He also missed.

"Shit!" screamed Smith. "Bank right, then cut back left. Let's see if we can fake him out."

The chopper jockeys tilted right and the gunship swung left. Smith fired again. This time the tracers passed right through the open doors, taking one of the gunship's door gunners with them. In the excitement of the chase, Smith's pilot had forgotten about the ground battle and passed too low over Parros's troops, who opened up on the chopper. Bullets clanked against the steel protecting the underbelly of the Huey.

"Get it up, Cowboy! Get us up!" yelled Smith.

Cowboy pulled back on the stick and nosed the bird upward, but not before a stray round ricocheted off one of the skids and tore through a fuel line. Gas spewed all over Smith and the floor of the chopper.

"We're hit! We're hit!" he yelled, as he left the guns and tried to find something to slow the leak.

The warning light flashed on the pilot's panel. The chopper jockey yelled into his mike, "Bird Dog Two. This is One. We're hit and losing fuel fast. He's all yours! Out."

Parros's gunship saw the chopper was in trouble and tried to swing in low underneath to get a shot. It was a mistake. The Ecuadorian pilot looked down at his firing switch then back up, just in time to see the tracer rounds of the fifties from the second chopper coming straight at him. The first round tore his head off and the next five exploded the bird in midair.

Jake and his men cheered wildly at the sight of the fireball in the sky. Then he realized he didn't have a radio with which to direct the fire of the U.S. chopper. Turning quickly to locate the one that had been lying in the open, he saw it had been destroyed by the first gun run. He knew the chopper wouldn't fire into the forest without radio contact. He was right.

They watched silently as the bird turned toward the town and departed. But at least they didn't have to worry about the gunships any more. The air show over, Parros's men renewed their fire on the few remaining survivors on the east slope. Mortimer looked around in despair. They were down to only sixteen men and the ammo was running low. Of the twenty-four men of 772 and 776, only nine were still alive. Only six of Escobar's rugged little SF band remained.

The battlefield fell silent for a few minutes. Jake knew they were getting ready to assault the team in force. He figured they were outnumbered at least four to one. He smiled to himself as he suddenly thought that a desk job would look pretty fucking good right now. Jake turned to tell his men to get ready, but found words were not necessary. The men were laying what few magazines they had left on the ground next to them. Bayonets were locked into place on their rifles and knives stuck in the dirt next to the magazines for easy access when the bullets ran out. This was what it was all about, this was the true meaning of the profession of arms. No matter what country, what army, or what people. For those who chose it, this moment would always come. Jake pulled the long K-Bar blade from its carrier and stuck it in the ground, then tried to remember if he had ever sent those flowers to that airline stewardess before he left.

Parros's men wanted this thing over with. They had already taken more casualties than Rivas had said they would. Of the one hundred at the ambush site, seventy remained. Surely enough to finish off the enemy rabble. The captain in charge spread his forces on line. They would make one mass attack and sweep over the few survivors, then be done with it. Raising his arm, the captain yelled at the top of his lungs and seventy screaming commandos charged down the hill and across the clearing, heading straight for Mortimer and his men.

Jake picked out a target and took up the slack in his trigger.

"Steady boys. Let's let 'em get bunched up in that clearing. Steady, steady. Make every shot count."

Jake sighted in on the second button on the target's shirt. A grin suddenly came across his face as he thought of his grandmother, and what she would tell people at the funeral. He could just hear her sweet old crackling voice as she said, "I told them he had brain damage. Too much football." The more he thought about it, the funnier it became, until he was laughing so loud the others broke out in laughter too. As they laughed the commandos drew closer.

"Fire!" yelled Jake as he pulled the trigger and sent the second button of a man's shirt through his chest and out his back.

The small battlefield erupted in gunfire, explosions, and screams as if hell itself were opening up right before their eyes. Jake dropped a third empty magazine and reached for another. They were gone. One by one, his men fired their last rounds, and, laying their rifles aside, pulled their knives from the ground and prepared to take someone to hell with them.

Jake and his men were totally unprepared for the thunderous volley of gunfire that suddenly erupted from both sides of them. The commandos were caught in a murderous crossfire from the ridges to the north and south.

In a matter of sixty seconds, it was all over. Seventy men lay dead or dying in the small clearing. Gradually the moans stopped and only a twitching hand or foot was all that remained of their lives.

The Special Forces soldiers were stunned. They couldn't believe what they had just seen happen. Jake stood and looked to the north, then the south. He couldn't see anyone. Turning back toward his men, he froze. There, standing on the high ground above them were the guerrillas. He guessed there were as many as a hundred. Their guns were leveled at Jake and his men. The small spark of hope that had consumed them all only moments ago now faded. Jake dropped his knife and considered going for the pistol that lay only a few feet away. Hell, he didn't even know if it had a round left in it.

"Don't be a foolish man, gringo!" said one of the guerrillas who stood on an outcropping of rocks above them. "I have no desire to kill you, or your brave men. Please be so kind as to drop your weapons and move over here."

Jake saw no point in offering any resistance now. He signaled the men to do as they were told. Now that they were where he wanted them, the man came down from the rocks and stood in front of Mortimer. Studying the commander for a moment, he turned and walked among the captured men, counting them as he did. Returning to Mortimer, he offered Jake his canteen. Jake reached for it, then stopped and looked back at his men. They had shed their rucksacks when the firefight started. No one had any water.

The Cuban leader nodded to his men, who pulled their canteens and offered them to the prisoners. While they drank, the leader went over, sat down on a log, and wondered to himself why life had to be so difficult, why some things just never seemed to work out right. While the men drank their water, Joaquin Ochoa tried to figure out what he was going to do with ten American and six Ecuadorian soldiers.

Colonel Ramon Escobar and Major Mattson listened as Captain William (Cowboy) Copus and Master Sergeant Smith concluded their story of the helicopter dogfight that had taken place in the mountains to the east. They could confirm there were KIAs. Smith and the crew had seen the bodies littering the ground, but at no time had they been able to establish contact with their ground forces. Could they identify the enemy forces? No, but there had seemed to be an awful lot of Ecuadorian troops in the area. Mattson was trying to maintain his professional composure, but his concern for Jake and the SF Teams had him on the verge of screaming for someone to do something.

Colonel Escobar was just as concerned as Mattson, but he also had four different situations on his hands at the same time. He was under orders from President Pizarro to halt the escape from the country of those who had been identified in Highfield's list. He had to organize, plan, and conduct an assault on the Parros ranch, and at the same time rescue Paul Bracken from the island of Genovesa, and save what remained of the SF unit in the mountains. All told, that was a hell of a big order to put on one man. Yet Escobar was attempting to handle it all. Things were being made more difficult by the fact that attempts to coordinate joint operations with other Ecuadorian units required authorization from the units' commanders. They, of course, were not available, because they were on Highfield's list and were trying to flee the country.

It was Highfield who finally came up with the answer. Why not have President Pizarro make Escobar temporary commander in chief of all Ecuadorian military forces? That would eliminate the middle men. If Escobar gives an order, you do it. That simple.

The colonel was on the phone. Within minutes Highfield's plan had been approved by Pizarro. An executive order would be cut and distributed to all commands within the hour. In a country where military takeovers happened all too often, a simple phone call from the President was not good enough. The graveyards of Latin America were filled with officers who had taken only someone's word.

Colonel Powers was on the phone. He needed to speak to Mattson. It was urgent. Highfield called B.J. to the phone, then joined Escobar at the map of Parros's ranch and the surrounding area. Although still in the country unofficially, Highfield had volunteered to lead the assault on Parros's ranch while Mattson and Escobar handled the rescue of Mortimer and the Special Forces Teams.

Mattson finished his conversation and joined them at the map board.

"Colonel, looks like you're going to have to pull Jake's ass out of the fire by yourself. That was Colonel Powers at the embassy. He was aware of the possibility that the consul general was being held on the island of Genovesa, so he contacted General Johnson and received authorization to divert a U.S. Navy SEAL Team from their training mission in Costa Rica to help us out. They're at the Embassy now. If you'll write me out an authorization to utilize a couple of your Ecuadorian SEAL Teams and a chinook helicopter, SEAL Team Five and I will take care of that problem for you."

General Sweet entered the Special Operations communications room and checked the information coming over the teletype. President Pizarro's request for a forty-eight-hour delay had upset his plan of operation. The 82nd Airborne commander was still holding at condition yellow and Pope Air Wing had all necessary C-130s available for instant lift-off. All they were waiting for was the go signal from Sweet. Surprisingly, General Johnson had been rather pleasant to him in the last twenty-four hours. He had given him a free hand in organizing and planning the operation from the very beginning, and had even encouraged the NSC and the joint chiefs to adopt his plan, a point that had also surprised a number of them, while still others sensed a trap in the making. No matter. Even the President of Ecuador would have to bend to the pressure if the situation became any worse.

Moving to one of the communications consoles operated by one of his informants, Sweet asked, "Any new developments, Sergeant?"

Some of the other operators in the room looked in their direction, waiting for the man to answer. They were all aware of Sweet's purpose at SOCOM and resented him for it. General Johnson was a fine officer and they were loyal to him, to the last man. Or so they thought.

The young sergeant replied in a loud and clear voice, "No, sir. Everything is still the same." At the same time he gave his answer, he slid a copy of the SEAL request into the stack of papers Sweet had put on the console.

Picking up the papers, Sweet answered, "Fine, Sergeant. Thank you. If anything should come in, please let me know." With that, he left the room and secured the door. The other operators gave the thumbs up to their fellow communicator.

Alone in his office, Sweet read the request Powers had sent to divert the SEAL Team. So Johnson wasn't playing all his cards above the table. He wondered if his superiors in Washington had been alerted to this latest development. Picking up the phone, he had begun to make the call when his sergeant from the radio room opened the door, then, looking over his shoulder to assure that he had not been seen, stepped into the office and closed the door.

"Sorry, General. But I thought you'd better see this right away. It just came in over the secure SITCOM frequency from our number two satellite. Looks like our boys are getting their asses kicked. One helicopter shot up and at least nine or ten SF guys killed. I gotta get back, sir. You won't forget my assignment to Hawaii, will you, sir?"

"You'll have the orders within twenty-four hours, my boy. Thank you. Thank you very much."

Sweet quickly read the classified message from Powers. This was it. This was all he would need to launch the 82nd. Punching the buttons on the phone that would give him the NSC hot line, he waited as the receptionist tried to locate his superior. She came back on the line.

"I'm sorry, sir. They are with the President and cannot take any calls at this time. If you like, I can take a message and see that it is delivered to whomever you like in the conference."

"No. No messages. Can't you patch me through for only a minute?"

"I am sorry, sir."

Sweet was in a dilemma. He was positive that Johnson had no intention of releasing this message to the joint chiefs or the NSC. Powers had noted at the end of the message that steps were being taken to save the situation. But yet he couldn't have some receptionist walking into the middle of a presidential briefing to deliver a classified message of this nature. The President would want to know where it came from, plus it would finger Sweet's boss within the NSC. No. That was no good. He hung up and considered his options. They had told him to use his judgment if something like this should ever happen. That was exactly what he was going to do. Removing a ring of keys from his pocket, he unlocked the right-hand drawer and removed a cream-colored phone with multicolored push buttons. Punching the red key, he listened as a long continuous ring came over the line.

Someone answered, "G-2. Eighty-second Airborne Division, sir."

Sweet's voice was a little shaky, but the words were clear

and concise. "Green on blue. Six-four-niner. The sky is falling."

"Confirm. Green on blue. Six-four-niner. The sky is falling."

"Roger. Confirmed," said Sweet.

"Roger, out," replied an excited voice at the other end of the line.

Replacing the phone in the drawer, he locked it and walked to the window. Within twenty minutes the first lift of the 82nd Airborne Division would be in the air and headed for Ecuador. Even General Johnson could not hide the total annihilation of two complete A-Teams for very long. When it was exposed, an all-out deployment would be called and he would be the one who would receive the praise of President and superiors alike for his insight and taking the initiative in a national crisis. While Johnson was certain to be asked to resign.

Major Ochoa walked up to Mortimer and asked, "Are you the commander of this unit?"

"I am now," he replied.

"Could I speak to you a moment in private?"

The rest of the team was sitting in a circle, surrounded by guerrillas. The sole surviving medic was treating the wounded, assisted by two of Ochoa's men.

"Well, Major, I suppose right about now you can do just about anything you please. Sure, I'd be interested to find out why in hell you haven't killed all of us yet."

Ochoa could sense the resentment in Jake's voice. But looking at the dead Americans lying below, it was a resentment he could understand.

The two officers moved away from the group and stood at the edge of the trees. The Cuban commander offered a cigarette. Jake turned it down.

"Where's Paul Bracken? Or have you already killed him?"

"If he is dead, commander, it is not we who are to blame, just as so many of the other things that have happened in the past forty-eight hours. The killing of the two American civilians, the killing of the Ecuadorian soldiers, the attack on the oilfield; and it should be obvious even to you now that we had nothing to do with the ambush of you and your men. If we had done all these things, why are you not dead now?"

"That's a good fucking question, Poncho!"

"The name is Ochoa, Commander. Major Joaquin Ochoa."

"OK, Ochoa. I guess next you're going to tell me you didn't kill Garces or kidnap the consul general, either, right?"

"No, that I must admit was our work. We had gone to kidnap the fat man, but unfortunately, for reasons I will not go into, I killed the bastard. Your Mister Bracken happened by, so I took him instead. A major—how do you Americans put it? Oh yes—a major fuck up on my part. But I assure you commander, we attempted to return Mr. Bracken immediately. No one was more surprised that he was still missing than we were."

Jake thought about what the man was saying. It almost made sense. Why would these people save his men if they intended to kill them later anyway? All in all, this guy Ochoa didn't seem to be such a bad fellow. Why would he lie? There wasn't anything to gain by it.

"So what you're saying is, you guys came in here to start a revolution but you really haven't done anything bad. Is that it?"

Ochoa laughed for a moment. "I suppose you could put it that way. As a matter of fact, Commander, my fuck-up with Bracken has resulted in putting an end to the planned revolution. You see, we have been ordered to withdraw from this country. That is what we were doing when we heard the firefight begin."

Jake's opinion of the man was improving every minute. Ochoa hadn't had to tell him that, but he had. "Well let me ask you something, Major. It must have been pretty confusing coming up on a firefight and seeing Ecuadorian soldiers shooting the hell out of Americans and other Ecuadorian troops. How'd you happen to pick our side?"

Smiling, Ochoa pointed to one of Parros's dead soldiers.

"It was easy, Commander. Do you see that patch on the man's shoulder? These men belong to a general named Parros. He and his men slaughtered a small group of my people not long ago. We found three of them hanging from a tree, their legs cut off. No, it was not a hard decision for me or my men to decide who we would help."

"So, what happens to us now?" asked Jake.

Ochoa crushed his cigarette out with his boot and waved for his commo man to join them.

"Commander—I'm sorry, would you mind telling me your name?"

"Mortimer. Lieutenant Commander Jake Mortimer."

"Mortimer? A very unusual name. However, Commander Mortimer. I am prepared to offer you a deal, as one officer to another. Please hear me out. If we can agree, then so be it."

"Like I said, Major, you hold all the cards. Please continue."

"Well, I assume that the helicopters which returned to town have alerted Colonel Escobar as to the seriousness of your situation. It is also feasible to assume that within the next thirty minutes or so Colonel Escobar will arrive with a large airmobile force to assist you. As I have said, we are withdrawing from Ecuador and neither I nor my men wish to engage in a full scale battle with Escobar. Had we not stopped to save you and your men, it is likely we would have already crossed the river into Columbia and be safely on our way home. Unfortunately that is not the case. Due to the time we have lost here, Colonel Escobar can now cut us off from our escape route and possibly surround us. Therefore, Commander, I will give you this radio, with which you can direct the evacuation and extraction of your people, in exchange for your word that you will not reveal the direction in which we have gone. We shall only need one hour to reach the river. If you can do this thing then you and your men can have the radio and retain all your weapons as well. That is the deal, Commander."

Jake had watched Ochoa's eyes as the man spoke. Mortimer considered himself a pretty good judge of character. This man was speaking the truth. They were tired of fighting and wanted only to go home. What was wrong with that?

"How do you know I will keep my word, Major Ochoa?"

"Just as you are judging me now, I have already judged you, commander. I believe we are both professionals. In this wretched time our word is the only thing that we truly have of any value. To give it is to make a decision free of influence from those who control us. If you give me your word on this matter, Commander Mortimer, then I will not question it, and my men and I will leave."

Jake vowed to remember those words. Smiling, he reached out his hand to grasp that of the Cuban officer.

"You have my word, Major Ochoa. And good luck to you and your men."

"Thank you, Commander. I shall not forget you. Who knows? One day we may meet again."

"Under different circumstances, I hope."

"I too, Commander. May God go with you," said Joaquin.

Instructing his commo man to leave the radio, Ochoa yelled for his troops to move out. As they crested the hill, Ochoa turned back and waved good-bye to the American commander; then they were gone.

The Green Beret medic looked up from his work as Jake stood above him waving.

"God, I can't believe they didn't kill us. I wonder why?" he said.

"There are still some men of honor left in this profession, Sergeant. We were just fortunate to have met one of them."

Within twenty minutes, Colonel Escobar and his airmobile force landed at an LZ just beyond Jake's position. He established contact and informed them the area was safe, and that they needed stretchers and a large supply of body bags. Escobar came up the hill and surveyed the battlefield. The question of guerrillas never came up and neither Jake nor any of the survivors planned to mention it.

B.J. shifted in the web seat fastened along the wall of the Chinook helicopter, trying to find a comfortable position. This was impossible with all the equipment he was wearing. Strapped across his chest was a LARV-5 Draeger, a front-mounted rebreathing rig. It had replaced the reserve parachute he was used to wearing in the position. Along his right side was strapped a waterproof kit bag containing his CAR-15 automatic rifle. Hanging below the Draeger there was another waterproof bag with loaded magazines and hand grenades. Finally there were the fins taped securely to the outside of his legs, just above the ankles. Uncomfortable was not the word that came to B.J.'s mind at the moment. This was fucked up. Here he was, a combat infantry officer, getting ready to take the plunge with a bunch of Navy SEALs, while the Navy guy was in a shoot-out in the middle of the Goddamned jungle. It was just all backasswards.

Looking up from his continued agony, he looked down the line of Navy divers. Most of the Ecuadorian teams and a few of Team Five were trying to get a little sleep. It was going to be a long swim. Sitting directly across from him was Chief Petty Officer Bob Nelson, the SEAL Team leader, smiling and shaking his head. No doubt he too was wondering what in hell an infantry officer was doing in this Draeger getup. Next to Nelson, sat Petty Officer 1st Class Brian Chambers, the assistant team leader. He had been the one to check Mattson out on the Draeger. B.J. was scuba qualified, but that had been a long time ago. He had found out quickly that the gear had changed considerably. He had never seen one of these rebreathing outfits before, let alone used one. Chambers had told him the only thing he had to be careful of was a "caustic cocktail."

That was something that would happen if his rig became flooded. He'd be able to tell when it happened, because the chemicals in the tank, when mixed with water, gave off a nasty mixture of fumes that caused an extremely bad taste and mild burns in the diver's mouth. In a serious case of flooding a diver could die from the caustic fumes burning his lungs. Now, that was a happy thought.

B.J. had to admit that these guys had been more than patient with him, answering all his questions and trying to assure him he would be fine. Smashing himself deeper into the webbing, Mattson still wished it was Jake here instead of him.

Powers had radioed the helicopter that the A-Teams had taken a beating but that Jake was all right. He, Highfield, and Colonel Escobar were already on their way to the Parros ranch for the final showdown. All that remained now was the rescue of Paul Bracken.

Mattson had briefed the SEAL Team on the situation, and a study of the terrain on Genovesa showed that only the west end of the island provided enough cover and conceal-ment for anyone to hide in that didn't want to be seen by overflying aircraft or passing ships. They planned to fly within two miles of the island, where the chopper would drop to within twenty feet of the ocean and they would exit off the rear ramp. The chopper would then turn back for Ecuador. Special boat units were already en route and would pick them up after they had secured Bracken and neutralized the island. Once in the water, they would slip on their fins and swim above water until they were within a quarter mile of land. They would cover that final distance underwater, using the Draegers.

The Ecuadorian crew chief signaled they were ready to drop down on the deck. SEAL Team Five stood up and made its way to the back ramp. Mattson fell in at the rear of the pack. He would go last. That way if he got in trouble the team would already be in the water and could help him.

Nelson gave the team the thumbs up sign, then leaned out over the side of the ramp. Looking back at the crew chief, he waved his hand in a downward motion. The chief relayed the request to go lower to the pilots. Satisfied that they were low enough for a safe leap, he pointed Chambers to go.

In less than ten seconds they were all in the water. Mattson came up spitting salt water and feeling the spray from the down wash of the helicopter against his face. The Chinook lifted and swung away toward home. Struggling in the choppy water, B.J. finally managed to get the fins on his feet. Signaling he was all right and ready to go, they began the two mile swim toward Genovesa. Mattson found that he was actually enjoying this. The only thing that kept both-

ering him was a crystal clear vision of the movie, *Jaws*. He
tried not to think about it.

Stroke after stroke Mattson kept watching the bobbing
heads of the others. One mile gone, one to go. His legs felt
like lead. He tried to think of Florida, of Charlotte and the
kids. Anything to take his mind off the legs and aching
arms. Now he remembered why he had joined the Army. He
could walk a hell of a lot farther than he could swim.

Suddenly there was the island. Nelson stopped swimming
and signaled for them to go to the Draegers. Mattson placed
the mouthpiece in his mouth, hit the switch, and went
down. At first he had a hard time breathing and nearly lost
it. Two members of Team Five were at his side immediately, signaling for him to relax and let it flow smoothly.
After three or four more breaths, he was fine. The SEALs
flanked him as they fell in behind the others.

It would have been better if they were under cover of
darkness, but that wasn't the case. Mattson could see the
sandy bottom coming up below him. They were only fifty
yards from the shoreline. Nelson had briefed the Ecuadorians that once they were at this distance, they were to go on
line on each side of the American team. He and Chambers
would be the only two to go to the surface. If it was clear,
Chambers would bring the rest of them up. They had no
idea how many of Parros's men were on the island. They
had to be ready for anything.

Mattson watched the two leaders go to the surface.
Nelson moved out of his view. Chambers was still near the
top, treading water. It seemed to take hours, but it was a
minute before Chambers came back down and waved them
up. Nelson was already near the trees, his MP-5 out of
the case and a magazine locked in place. He signaled the
Ecuadorian team on the left to exit first. Then the one on the
right. Finally he looked at Mattson and waved them

forward. Shedding all but their ammo bags and weapons, they moved out. Two of the men from Team Five took the point, while the other teams covered the flanks. Slowly they moved over the hard volcanic rock and ash of the island that had been formed centuries ago.

The point men stopped and dropped to the ground. One held up four fingers and indicated bad guys were coming their way. Mattson and the others spread out. Drawing their knives, the SEALs waited until the four men were in the middle of them before leaping up, cutting their throats, and lowering them to the ground.

Moving again, they had only gone twenty yards when the point again dropped and waved the commanders forward. Nelson looked at Mattson and motioned for him to follow. Staying low along the small ridge of sand, they peered over at the camp. There were five large tents spread over an area of fifty yards. The three larger tents had the side flaps lifted to allow what air there was to circulate among the cots. Most of the men were sleeping. Their weapons leaned against the trees or next to their cots.

Mattson searched the area until he found what he was looking for. Tapping Nelson on the arm, he pointed to a small hut that sat among the trees to the east. The front was open, and Paul Bracken sat cross-legged, his hands tied behind his back and a blindfold over his eyes. Nelson nodded and motioned for them to fall back. As the teams gathered around, Nelson asked, "How do you want to do this?"

"Your teams, your show, Chief. You call it," said Mattson.

"Be a hell of a lot simpler if it were nighttime, but we can't wait. The special boat boys will be here in an hour. We've got to do it now. Chambers, what do you think?" asked Nelson.

"Well, they have Bracken away from the main group. That should keep him out of the line of fire if we go in hard and hot," replied the executive officer.

"I agree. Okay, that's how we play it. We take 'em down hard!" Looking over at their counterparts, Nelson said, "Duro!" They smiled and nodded their approval. Mattson, Chambers, and two of the Ecuadorians were to maneuver around to where Bracken was. When the firing started, they would pull him to safety and take on any targets of opportunity. The others were to spread out around the camp and when Nelson threw the first grenade the show would be on. "Okay, let's nail their ass, Navy," said Nelson, as they took their positions.

Nelson had given them five minutes to get into position. Looking at his watch, he pulled the pin on a grenade. As the sweep hand swung up on twelve, he arched his arm and let the grenade fly. The charging handle popped, then flew off as the small round ball of death hit the ground and exploded. The four men standing by the campfire were blown off their feet. Two were dead, the others screaming and whimpering in pain from the shrapnel that had torn through their bodies.

At the sound of the explosion the SEALs jumped to their feet and, screaming at the top of their lungs, charged over the sand dunes, firing at everything that moved. Mattson stood up next to a tree and fired a short burst into the two soldiers guarding Bracken. Chambers dived into the small hut and grabbed the consul general under his arms and pulled him to safety behind Mattson and the two Ecuadorians, now laying down a murderous fire.

The soldiers sleeping in the tents scrambled for their weapons but were cut down before they could raise them. Mattson saw two soldiers suddenly appear from the direction of the beach. One kneeled and fired a single shot that hit Nelson square in the back. The chief's body went rigid for a moment as he screamed, "Oh shit!" then fell dead in the sand. Chambers had seen his leader go down. Screaming, he pulled his knife, and firing his MP-5 with one hand he killed one of the men. The man who had fired the fatal shot dropped his gun in terror and tried to run away. Chambers tossed his weapon to the side and leaped on the man's back, dragging him to the ground. B.J. saw the knife go high in the air and come down hard, over and over again.

By the time it was over. All but three of Parros's commandos were dead. Friendly losses had been one U.S. killed, two wounded, four Ecuadorians killed and three wounded. Paul Bracken was all right, a little shaken by all the gunfire and the sight of the dead, but other than that he was fine. He told Mattson that he had never doubted for a minute that he would be rescued. As the boats arrived to take them off the island, Bracken had a thousand questions. Mattson told him he would try to answer them all on the trip back.

Mortimer, Highfield, and "General" Escobar were waiting for them as the helicopter that had picked them up on the coast landed in President Pizarro's courtyard. Powers and the ambassador were there, as well as every dignitary in the government. Pizarro came forward and hugged both men as he praised the actions of the Americans which had led to Bracken's rescue and the expulsion of the corrupt element within his new government.

B.J. shook hands with Bracken, then made his way out of the crowd to where Mortimer and the newly appointed chief of staff stood. Escobar wrapped his arm around Mattson as he congratulated him on the success of his mission.

Jake smiled half heartedly and shook his hand. Mattson

could see the sadness in his partner's eyes, as he said, "Pretty rough, huh?"

"Yeah, and damn costly, too. Want me to tell you about it?"

"No, not right now. I'd rather enjoy a moment of feeling like it was all worth it." Pausing a moment, B.J. asked, "Did you get Parros?"

Jake's head seemed to droop clear to the concrete. Highfield answered the question for him.

"The bastard got away, B.J. Don't ask me how. We had the place surrounded so tight a fucking chipmunk couldn't have gotten out of there without us seeing him. I just don't figure it. Cleaned house on the rest of them though. Escobar used the Air Force to level the place. Don't think we had more than twenty prisoners out of the whole mess."

Powers came over and, slapping Mattson on his sore shoulders, said, "Hell of a job, son. I called the White House as soon as the boats radioed the news that you had Bracken. The President was delighted. Told me to thank you for him personally. He plans to have Paul Bracken flown to Washington as soon as he is able to travel. He is very pleased with the way this matter was handled and has invited General Johnson to the White House to discuss additional funding for Special Operations."

"How'd General Sweet take the news?" asked Mattson.

Jake smiled for the first time, as Powers burst out in a wild laugh. "Oh, brother. Did he step on his crank! He was burning up the airwaves with recall codes to damn near everybody. The commander of the 82nd is screaming for an investigation and the defense secretary has told him to get to Washington. There's a little matter of who's going to pay for a shit load of C-130 fuel."

As Powers was telling his story, B.J. saw one of Escobar's officers rush up to the general and point toward the main gate of the courtyard. There stood two tall Jivaro Indians, their bodies painted with the traditional stripes of their ancestors. Each wore only a loin cloth with a bright red sash tied around the waist. General Escobar and the officer went to them, spoke for a moment, then the Indians handed him a bag and departed. Escobar now came to where they were standing.

Powers had just finished talking. Opening the bag, Escobar reached in and removed the head of General Arturo Parros. Holding it by the hair, he said, "The Jivaros found the graves of the young girls from their village. They blamed this man for their deaths and wanted you to have this in honor of all you have done here."

The Americans looked at the head with the staring eyes as Mattson said, "Thanks, General, but I don't think it'll go with my furniture."

"I thought not," said Escobar with a smile as he placed the head back in the bag, and he and the other officer walked away.

Highfield's eyes suddenly widened as he asked, "Major, you sure you don't want that?"

They were all staring at the CIA man as B.J. replied, "Absolutely positive. Just something else Charlotte would have to dust."

"All right!" yelled Highfield with excitement as he turned and ran after Escobar. "Hey, General! Wait a minute!"

Powers shook his head, then said, "You both should be proud of the job you've done here." Shaking their hands once more, Powers smiled. "Well, I've got to go. Colonel—or I should say General Escobar—wants me to join him, the ambassador, and President Pizarro for supper tonight."

Jake's face went crimson with rage as Powers walked

away. "So that's it huh? A lot of slaps on the back and toothy grins, dished out with a lot of thank yous, and great job crap! Shit, B.J., they're having fucking celebration dinners and all night parties! What about the guys who paid the price for all this shit? Huh? What about them? What about Hay and Cleveland, the sergeant major? What about them?"

"Easy, Jake, it comes with the territory. Hell, if it was easy, everybody would want to be doing it."

"Damn it, B.J., it's just not right. How do you stand it? Aren't you pissed? Even a little mad?"

"No, not really, Jake. I learned how it works a long time ago after Vietnam. At least they said thanks for this one. You ready to go home?" he asked, as he walked away, without waiting for Jake's answer.

Mortimer hadn't been sure he could handle this job after what he had seen today. But with a guy like B.J. around, he was going to learn a lot. Running to catch up, he yelled, "Hey, B.J.! Did I call a flower shop while we were at the club the other night?"

HIGH-TECH ADVENTURES BY BESTSELLING AUTHORS

__**TEAM YANKEE** by Harold Coyle
0-425-11042-7/$4.95
Live the first two weeks of World War III through the eyes of tank team commander Captain Sean Bannon, as he and his soldiers blast their way across the war-torn plains of Europe.

__**AMBUSH AT OSIRAK** by Herbert Crowder
0-515-09932-5/$4.50
Israel is poised to attack the Iraqi nuclear production plant at Osirak. But the Soviets have supplied Iraq with the ultimate super-weapon . . . and the means to wage nuclear war.

__**SWEETWATER GUNSLINGER 201** by Lt. Commander William H. LaBarge and Robert Lawrence Holt 1-55773-191-8/$4.50
Jet jockeys Sweetwater and Sundance are the most outrageous pilots in the skies. Testing the limits of their F-14s and their commanding officers, these boys won't let anything get in the way of their fun!

__**WILDCAT** by Craig Thomas 0-515-10186-9/$4.95
Crossing the globe from Moscow to London to East Berlin to Katmandu, the bestselling author of *Winter Hawk* delivers edge-of-the-seat suspense spiked with state-of-the-art espionage gadgetry.